This season Harlequin® Romance brings you

Christmas Treats

For an extra-special treat this Christmas
don't look under the Christmas tree or in
your stocking—pick up one of your favorite
Harlequin Romance novels, curl up and relax!

From presents to proposals, mistletoe to marriage,
we promise to deliver seasonal warmth, wonder
and of course the unbeatable rush of romance!

*And look out for Christmas surprises
this month in Harlequin Romance!*

For the photo shoot Cassie was setting a round table as if for a wedding reception, and Jake was astounded by the detail.

"How on earth did you think of all this?" he asked.

"All I had to do in this case was act out a fantasy I've had for years," Cassie said cheerfully. "I always wanted a Christmas wedding, and in my fantasy it was here at the hall, so I didn't really have to think of anything. I knew exactly what I wanted!"

"It does look surprisingly Christmassy," he said, looking around. "All you need is some mistletoe."

"It's too early, unfortunately, and don't think I haven't tried to get some!"

"Let's pretend it's hanging right here," he said, pointing above their heads and drawing Cassie to him with his other arm. "Then I can kiss you underneath it."

JESSICA HART
Under the Boss's Mistletoe

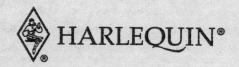

HARLEQUIN®

TORONTO • NEW YORK • LONDON
AMSTERDAM • PARIS • SYDNEY • HAMBURG
STOCKHOLM • ATHENS • TOKYO • MILAN • MADRID
PRAGUE • WARSAW • BUDAPEST • AUCKLAND

Recycling programs
for this product may
not exist in your area.

ISBN-13: 978-0-373-17624-3

UNDER THE BOSS'S MISTLETOE

First North American Publication 2009.

Copyright © 2009 by Jessica Hart.

This edition published by arrangement with Harlequin Books S.A.

® and TM are trademarks of the publisher. Trademarks indicated with
® are registered in the United States Patent and Trademark Office, the
Canadian Trade Marks Office and in other countries.

www.eHarlequin.com

Printed in U.S.A.

Jessica Hart was born in West Africa, and has suffered from itchy feet ever since, traveling and working around the world in a wide variety of interesting but very lowly jobs. All of them have provided inspiration on which to draw when it comes to the settings and plots of her stories. Now she lives a rather more settled existence in York, U.K., where she has been able to pursue her interest in history, although she still yearns sometimes for wider horizons. If you'd like to know more about Jessica, visit her Web site at www.jessicahart.co.uk.

PROLOGUE

'I WANT a word with you!'

Cassie almost fell down the steps in her hurry to catch Jake before he zoomed off like the coward he was. The stumble did nothing to improve her temper as she stormed over to where he had just got onto his motorbike.

He had been about to put on his helmet, but he paused at the sound of her voice. In his battered leathers, he looked as dark and mean as the machine he sat astride. There was a dangerous edge to Jake Trevelyan that Cassie normally found deeply unnerving, but today she was too angry to be intimidated.

'You broke Rupert's nose!' she said furiously.

Jake observed her approach through narrowed eyes. The estate manager's ungainly daughter had a wild mane of curls, a round, quirky face and a mouth that showed promise of an interesting woman to come. Right now, though, she was still only seventeen, and reminded him of an exuberant puppy about to fall over its paws.

Not such a friendly puppy today, he observed. The normally dreamy brown eyes were flashing with temper. It wasn't too hard to guess what had her all riled up; she must have just been to see her precious Rupert.

'Not quite such a pretty boy today, is he?' he grinned.

Cassie's fists clenched. 'I'd like to break *your* nose,' she said and Jake laughed mockingly.

'Have a go,' he offered.

'And give you the excuse to beat me up as well? I don't think so.'

'I didn't beat Rupert up,' said Jake dismissively. 'Is that what he told you?'

'I've just seen him. He looks *awful*.'

Cassie heard the crack in her voice and pressed her lips together in a fierce, straight line before she could humiliate herself utterly by bursting into tears.

She had been so happy, she had had to keep pinching herself. For as long as she could remember she had dreamed of Rupert, and now he was hers—or he had been. It was only three days since the ball, and he was in a vicious temper, which he'd taken out on her. It was all spoilt now.

And it was all Jake Trevelyan's fault.

'He's going to bring assault charges against you,' she told Jake, hoping to shock him, but he only looked contemptuous.

'So Sir Ian has just been telling me.'

Cassie had never understood why Sir Ian had so much time for a thug like Jake, especially now that he had beaten up his own nephew!

The Trevelyans were notorious in Portrevick for their shady dealings, and the only member of the family who had ever appeared to hold down a job at all was Jake's mother, who had cleaned for Sir Ian until her untimely death a couple of years ago. Jake himself had long had a reputation as a troublemaker. He was four years older than Cassie, and she couldn't remember a time when his dark, surly presence hadn't made him the kind of boy you crossed the road to avoid.

It was a pity she hadn't remembered that at the Allantide Ball.

Now Cassie glared at him, astonished by her own bravery. 'But then, I suppose the thought of prison wouldn't bother you,' she said. 'It's something of a family tradition, isn't it?'

Something unpleasant flared in Jake's eyes, and she took an involuntary step backwards, wondering a little too late whether she might have gone too far. There was a suppressed anger about him that should have warned her not to provoke him. She wouldn't put it past him to take out all that simmering resentment on her the way he so clearly had on Rupert, but in the end he only looked at her with dislike.

'What do you want, Miss Not-So-Goody Two Shoes?'

Cassie took a deep breath. 'I want to know why you hit Rupert.'

'Why does it matter?'

'Rupert said it was over me.' She bit her lip. 'He wouldn't tell me exactly what.'

Jake laughed shortly. 'No, I bet he wouldn't!'

'Was it…was it because of what happened at the Allantide Ball?'

'When you offered yourself to me on a plate?' he said, and her face flamed.

'I was just talking,' she protested, although she knew she had been doing more than that.

'You don't wear a dress like that just to *talk*,' said Jake.

Cassie's cheeks were as scarlet as the dress she had bought as part of a desperate strategy to convince Rupert that she had grown up.

Her parents had been aghast when they had seen it, and Cassie herself had been half-horrified, half-thrilled by how it had made her look. The colour was lovely—a deep, rich red—but it was made of cheap Lycra that had clung embarrassingly to every curve. Cut daringly short, it had such a low neckline that Cassie had had to keep tugging at it to stop herself spilling out. She cringed to think how fat and tarty she must have looked next to all those cool, skinny blondes dressed in black.

On the other hand, it had worked.

Rupert had definitely noticed her when she'd arrived, and that had given her the confidence to put Plan B into action. 'You need to make him jealous,' her best friend Tina had said. 'Make him realise that you're not just his for the taking—even if you are.'

Emboldened by Rupert's reaction, Cassie had smiled coolly and sashayed up to Jake instead. To this day, she didn't know where she had found the nerve to do it; he had been on his own for once, and watching the proceedings with a cynical air.

The Allantide Ball was a local tradition revived by Sir Ian, who had been obsessed by Cornish folklore. Less a formal ball than a big party, it was held in the Hall every year on 31st October, when the rest of the country was celebrating Hallowe'en, and everyone in Portrevick went, the one occasion when social divisions were put aside.

In theory, if not in practice.

Jake's expression had not been encouraging, but Cassie had flirted with him anyway. Or she had thought she was flirting. In retrospect, her heavy-handed attempts to bat her lashes and look sultry must have been laughable, but at the time she had been quite pleased with herself.

'OK, maybe I was flirting,' she conceded. 'That was no reason to…to…'

'To kiss you?' said Jake. 'But how else were you to make Rupert jealous? That *was* the whole point of the exercise, wasn't it?'

Taking Cassie's expression as an answer, he settled back into the saddle and regarded her with a mocking smile that made her want to slap him. 'It was a good strategy,' he congratulated her. 'Rupert Branscombe Fox is the kind of jerk who's only interested in what someone else has got. I'll bet even as a small boy he only ever wanted to play with someone else's toys. It was very astute of you to notice that.'

'I didn't.'

She had just wanted Rupert to notice her. Was that so bad? And he had. It had worked perfectly.

She just hadn't counted on Jake taking her flirtation so seriously. He had taken her by the hand and pulled her outside. Catching a glimpse of Rupert watching her, Cassie had been delighted at first. She'd been expecting a kiss, but not the kiss that she got.

It had begun with cool assurance—and, really, that would have been fine—but then something had changed. The coolness had become warmth, and then it had become heat, and then, worst of all, there had been a terrifying sweetness to it. Cassie had felt as if she were standing in a river with the sand rushing away beneath her feet, sucking her down into something wild and uncontrollable. She'd been terrified and exhilarated at the same time, and when Jake had let her go at last she had been shaking.

It wasn't even as if she liked Jake. He was the exact opposite of Rupert, who was the embodiment of a dream. Secretly, Cassie thought of them as Beauty and the Beast. Not that Jake was ugly, exactly, but he had dark, beaky features, a bitter mouth and angry eyes, while Rupert was all golden charm, like a prince in a fairy tale.

'Much good it'll do you,' Jake was saying, reading her expression without difficulty. 'You're wasting your time. Rupert's never going to bother with a nice girl like you.'

'Well, that's where you're wrong,' said Cassie, stung. 'Maybe I *did* want to make him notice me, but it worked, didn't it?'

'You're not asking me to believe that you're Rupert's latest girlfriend?'

Cassie lifted her chin. 'Believe what you want,' she said. 'It happens to be true.'

But Jake only laughed. 'Having sex with Rupert doesn't make you his girlfriend, as you'll soon find out,' he said. He reached for his helmet again. 'You need to grow up, Cassie. You've wandered around with your head in the clouds ever since you were a little kid, and it looks like you're still living in a fantasy world. It's time you woke up to reality!'

'You're just jealous of Rupert!' Cassie accused him, her voice shaking with fury.

'Because of you?' Jake raised his dark brows contemptuously. 'I don't think so!'

'Because he's handsome and charming and rich and Sir Ian's nephew, while you're just…just…' Too angry and humiliated to be cautious, she was practically toe to toe with him by now. 'Just an *animal*.'

And that was when Jake really did lose the temper he had been hanging onto by a thread all day. His hands shot out and yanked Cassie towards him so hard that she fell against him. Luckily his bike was still on its stand, or they would both have fallen over.

'So you think I'm jealous of Rupert, do you?' he snarled, shoving his hands into the mass of curls. 'Well, maybe I am.'

He brought his mouth down on hers in a hard, punishing kiss that had her squirming in protest, her palms jammed against his leather jacket, until abruptly the pressure softened.

His lips didn't leave hers, but he shifted slightly so that he could draw her more comfortably against him as he sat astride the bike. The fierce grip on her hair had loosened, and now her curls were twined around his fingers as the kiss grew seductively insistent.

Cassie's heart was pounding with that same mixture of fear and excitement, and she could feel herself losing her footing again. A surge of unfamiliar feeling was rapidly uncoiling inside her, so fast in fact that it was scaring her; her fingers curled instinctively into his leather jacket to anchor herself.

And then—the bit that would make her cringe for years afterwards—somehow she actually found herself leaning into him to kiss him back.

That was the point at which Jake let her go so abruptly that she stumbled back against the handlebars.

'How dare you?' Cassie managed, drawing a shaking hand across her mouth as she tried to leap away from the bike, only to find that her cardigan was caught up in the handlebars. Desperately, she tried to disentangle herself. 'I never want to see you again!'

'Don't worry, you won't have to.' Infuriatingly casual, Jake leant forward to pull the sleeve free; she practically fell back in her haste to put some distance between them. 'I'm leaving today. You stick to your fantasy life, Cassie,' he told her as she huddled into her cardigan, hugging her arms together. 'I'm getting out of here.'

And with that, he calmly fastened his helmet, kicked the bike off its stand and into gear and roared off down the long drive—leaving Cassie staring after him, her heart tumbling with shock and humiliation and the memory of a deep, dark, dangerous excitement.

CHAPTER ONE

Ten years later

'JAKE Trevelyan?' Cassie repeated blankly. 'Are you sure?'

'I wrote his name down. Where is it?' Joss hunted through the mess on her desk and produced a scrap of paper. 'Here— Jake Trevelyan,' she read. 'Somebody in Portrevick—isn't that where you grew up?—recommended us.'

Puzzled, Cassie dropped into the chair at her own desk. It felt very strange, hearing Jake's name after all this time. She could still picture him with terrifying clarity, sitting astride that mean-looking machine, an angry young man with hard hands and a bitter smile. The memory of that kiss still had the power to make her toes curl inside her shoes.

'He's getting married?'

'Why else would he get in touch with a wedding planner?'

'I just can't imagine it.' The Jake Trevelyan Cassie had known wasn't the type to settle down.

'Luckily for us, he obviously can.' Joss turned back to her computer. 'He sounded keen, anyway, so I said you'd go round this afternoon.'

'Me?' Cassie looked at her boss in dismay. 'You always meet the clients first.'

'I can't today. I've got a meeting with the accountant, which I'm not looking forward to at all. Besides, he knows you.'

'Yes, but he hates me!' She told Joss about that last encounter outside Portrevick Hall. 'And what's his fiancée going to think? I wouldn't want to plan my wedding with someone who'd kissed my bridegroom.'

'Teenage kisses don't count.' Joss waved them aside. 'It was ten years ago. Chances are, he won't even remember.'

Cassie wasn't sure if that would make her feel better or worse. She would just as soon Jake didn't remember the gawky teenager who had thrown herself at him at the Allantide Ball, but what girl wanted to know that she was utterly forgettable?

'Anyway, if he didn't like you, why ring up and ask to speak to you?' Joss asked reasonably. 'We can't afford to let a possible client slip through our fingers, Cassie. You know how tight things are at the moment. This is our best chance of new work in weeks, and if it means being embarrassed then I'm afraid you're going to have to be embarrassed,' she warned. 'Otherwise, I'm really not sure how much longer I'm going to be able to keep you on.'

Which was how Cassie came to stand outside a gleaming office-building that afternoon. Its windows reflected a bright September sky, and she had to crane her neck to look up to the top. Jake Trevelyan had done well for himself if he worked somewhere like this, she thought, impressed in spite of herself.

Better than she had, that was for sure, thought Cassie, remembering Avalon's chaotic office above the Chinese takeaway. Not that she minded. She had only been working for Joss a few months and she loved it. Wedding planning was far and away the best job she had ever had—Cassie had had a few, it had to be admitted—and she would do whatever it took to hang on to it. She couldn't bear to admit to her family of super-achievers that she was out of work.

Again.

'Oh, *darling*!' her mother would sigh with disappointment, while her father would frown and remind her that she should have gone to university like her elder sister and her two brothers, all of whom had high-flying careers.

No, she had to keep this job, Cassie resolved, and if that meant facing Jake Trevelyan again then that was what she would do.

Squaring her shoulders, she tugged her jacket into place and headed up the marble steps.

Worms were squirming in the pit of her stomach but she did her best to ignore them. It was stupid to be nervous about seeing Jake again. She wasn't a dreamy seventeen-year-old any longer. She was twenty-seven, and holding down a demanding job. People might not think that being a wedding planner was much of a career, but it required tact, diplomacy and formidable organizational-skills. If she could organise a wedding—well, help Joss organise one—she could deal with Jake Trevelyan.

A glimpse of herself in the mirrored windows reassured her. Luckily, she had dressed smartly to visit a luxurious hotel which one of their clients had chosen as a venue that morning. The teal-green jacket and narrow skirt gave her a sharp, professional image, Cassie decided, eyeing her reflection. Together with the slim briefcase, it made for an impressive look.

Misleading, but impressive. She hardly recognised herself, so with any luck Jake Trevelyan wouldn't recognise her either.

Her only regret was the shoes. It wasn't that they didn't look fabulous—the teal suede with a black stripe was perfect with the suit—but she wasn't used to walking on quite such high heels, and the lobby floor had an alarmingly, glossy sheen to it. It was a relief to get across to the reception desk without mishap.

'I'm looking for a company called Primordia,' she said, glancing down at the address Joss had scribbled down. 'Can you tell me which floor it's on?'

The receptionist lifted immaculate brows. 'This *is* Primordia,' she said.

'What, the whole building?' Cassie's jaw sagged as she

stared around the soaring lobby, taking in the impressive artwork on the walls and the ranks of gleaming lifts with their lights going up, up, up…

'Apparently he's boss of some outfit called Primordia,' Joss had said casually when she'd tossed the address across the desk.

This didn't look like an 'outfit' to Cassie. It looked like a solid, blue-chip company exuding wealth and prestige. Suddenly her suit didn't seem quite so smart.

'Um, I'm looking for someone called Jake Trevelyan,' she told the receptionist. 'I'm not sure which department he's in.'

The receptionist's brows climbed higher. 'Mr Trevelyan, our Chief Executive? Is he expecting you?'

Chief Executive? Cassie swallowed. 'I think so.'

The receptionist turned away to murmur into the phone while Cassie stood, fingering the buttons on her jacket nervously. Jake Trevelyan, bad boy of Portrevick, Chief Executive of all this?

Blimey.

An intimidatingly quiet lift took her up to the Chief Executive's suite. It was like stepping into a different world. Everything was new and of cutting-edge design, and blanketed with the hush that only serious money can buy.

It was a very long way from Portrevick.

Cassie was still half-convinced that there must be some mistake, but no. There was an elegant PA, who was obviously expecting her, and who escorted her into an impressively swish office.

'Mr Trevelyan won't be a minute,' she said.

Mr Trevelyan! Cassie thought of the surly tearaway she had known and tried not to goggle. She hoped Jake—sorry, *Mr Trevelyan*—didn't remember her flirting with him in that tacky dress or telling him that she never wanted to see him again. It wasn't exactly the best basis on which to build a winning client-relationship.

On the other hand, he was the one who had asked to see

her. Surely he wouldn't have done that if he had any memory of those disastrous kisses? Joss must be right; he had probably forgotten them completely. And, even if he hadn't, he was unlikely to mention that he had kissed her in front of his fiancée, wasn't he? He would be just as anxious as her to pretend that that had never happened.

Reassured, Cassie pinned on a bright smile as his PA opened a door into an even swisher office than the first. 'Cassandra Grey,' the woman announced.

It was a huge room, with glass walls on two sides that offered a spectacular view down the Thames to the Houses of Parliament and the London Eye.

Not that Cassie took in the view. She had eyes only for Jake, who was getting up from behind his desk and buttoning his jacket as he came round to greet her.

Her first thought was that he had grown into a surprisingly attractive man.

Ten years ago he had been a wiry young man, with turbulent eyes and a dangerous edge that had always left her tongue-tied and nervous around him. He was dark still, and there were traces of the difficult boy he had been in his face, but he had grown into the once-beaky features, and the surliness had metamorphosed into a forcefulness that was literally breathtaking. At least, Cassie presumed that was why she was having trouble dragging enough oxygen into her lungs all of a sudden.

He might not actually be taller, but he seemed it—taller, tougher, more solid somehow. And the mouth that had once been twisted into a sneer was now set in a cool, self-contained line.

Cassie was forced to revise her first thought. He wasn't attractive; he was *gorgeous*.

Well. Who would have thought it?

His fiancée was a lucky woman.

Keeping her smile firmly in place, she took a step towards

him with her hand outstretched. 'Hel…' she began, but that was as far as she got. Her ankle tipped over on the unfamiliar heels and the next moment her shoes seemed to be hopelessly entangled. Before Cassie knew what was happening, she found herself pitching forward with a squawk of dismay as her briefcase thudded to the floor.

She would have landed flat on her face next to it if a pair of hard hands hadn't grabbed her arms. Cassie had no idea how Jake got there in time to catch her, but she ended up sprawling against him and clutching instinctively at his jacket.

Just as she had clutched at his leather jacket ten years ago when he had kissed her.

'Hello, Cassie,' he said.

Mortified, Cassie struggled to find her balance. Why, why, *why*, was she so clumsy?

Her face was squashed against his jacket, and with an odd, detached part of her brain she registered that he smelt wonderful, of expensive shirts, clean, male skin and a faint tang of aftershave. His body was rock-solid, and for a treacherous moment Cassie was tempted to cling to the blissful illusion of steadiness and safety.

Possibly not a good move, if she wanted to impress him with her new-found professionalism. Or very tactful, given that he was a newly engaged man.

With an effort, Cassie pulled herself away from the comfort of that broad chest. 'I'm so sorry,' she managed.

Jake set her on her feet but kept hold of her upper arms until he was sure she was steady. 'Are you all right?'

His hands felt hard and strong through the sleeves of her jacket, and he held her just as he had done that other day.

Cassie couldn't help staring. It was strangely dislocating to look into his face and see a cool stranger overlaying the angry young man he had been then. This time the resentment in the dark-blue eyes had been replaced by a gleam of amusement, although it was impossible to tell whether he was remembering that kiss, too, or was simply entertained by her unconventional arrival.

Cassie's cheeks burned. 'I'm fine,' she said, stepping out of his grip.

Jake bent to pick up the briefcase and handed it back to her. 'Shall we sit down?' he suggested, gesturing towards two luxurious leather sofas. 'Given those shoes, it might be safer!'

Willing her flaming colour to fade, Cassie subsided onto a sofa and swallowed as she set the briefcase on the low table. 'I don't normally throw myself into the client's arms when we first meet,' she said with a nervous smile.

The corner of Jake's mouth quivered in an unnervingly attractive way. 'It's always good to make a spectacular entrance. But then, you always did have a certain style,' he added.

Cassie rather suspected that last comment was sarcastic; she had always been hopelessly clumsy.

She sighed. 'I was rather hoping you wouldn't recognise me,' she confessed.

Jake looked across the table at her. She was perched on the edge of the sofa, looking hot and ruffled, her round, sweet face flushed, and brown eyes bright with mortification.

The wild curls he remembered had been cut into a more manageable style, and she had slimmed down and smartened up. Remarkably so, in fact. When he had looked up to see her in the doorway, she had seemed a vividly pretty stranger, and he had felt a strange sensation in the pit of his stomach.

Then she had tripped and pitched into his arms, and Jake wasn't sure if he was disappointed or relieved to find out that she hadn't changed that much after all.

The feel of her was startlingly familiar, which was odd, given that he had only held her twice before. But he had caught her, and all at once it was as if he had been back at that last Allantide Ball. He could still see Cassie as she sashayed up to him in that tight red dress, teetering on heels almost as ridiculous as the ones she was wearing now, and suddenly all grown-up. That was the first time he had noticed her lush mouth, and wondered about the woman she would become.

That mouth was still the same, Jake thought, remembering its warmth, its innocence, remembering how unprepared he had been for the piercing sweetness that just for a moment had held them in its grip.

Now here she was again, sitting there and watching him with a wary expression in the big brown eyes. Not recognise her?

Jake smiled. 'Not a chance,' he said.

Oh dear. That wasn't what she had wanted to hear at all. Almost reluctantly, Cassie met the dark-blue gaze and felt her skin prickle at the amusement she read there. It was obvious that Jake remembered the gawky teenager she had been all too well. Those kisses might have been shattering for her, but for him they must have been just part of her gaucheness and lack of sophistication.

She lifted her chin. 'It's a long time ago,' she said. 'I didn't think you'd remember me.'

Jake met her eyes blandly. 'You'd be surprised what I remember,' he said, and the memory of the Allantide Ball was suddenly shimmering between them. He didn't have to say anything. Cassie just knew that he was remembering her hopeless attempts to flirt, and her clumsy, mortifyingly eager response to his kiss, and a tide of heat seemed to sweep up from her toes.

She jerked her eyes away. 'So,' she began, but all at once her voice was so high and thin that she had to clear her throat and start again. 'So...' Oh God, now she sounded positively gravelly! 'What took you back to Portrevick?' She managed to find something approaching a normal pitch at last. As far as she knew, Jake had left the village that awful day he had kissed her on his motorbike and had never been back.

Jake's expression sobered. 'Sir Ian's death,' he said.

'Oh yes, I was so sorry when I heard about that,' said Cassie, latching on to what she hoped would be a safe subject.

'He was such a lovely man,' she remembered sadly. 'Mum and Dad went back for the funeral, but one of our clients was getting married that day so I was on duty.'

The door opened at that point and Jake's PA came in with a tray of coffee which she set on the table between them. She poured two cups and made a discreet exit. Why could *she* never be that quiet and efficient? Cassie wondered, admiring the other woman's style.

Jake passed one of the cups to her, and she accepted it gingerly. It was made of the finest porcelain, and she couldn't help comparing it to the chipped mugs she and Joss used to drink endless cups of tea in the office.

'I had to go and see Sir Ian's solicitor on Friday,' Jake said, pushing the milk jug towards her. 'I stayed in the pub at Portrevick, and your name was mentioned in connection with weddings. One of your old friends—Tina?—said that you were in the business.'

'*Did* she?' Cassie made a mental note to ring Tina the moment she left and demand to know why she hadn't told her that Jake Trevelyan had reappeared. It wasn't as if Tina didn't know all about that devastating kiss at the Allantide Ball, although Cassie had never told anyone about the second one.

Jake raised his eyes a little at her tone, and she hastened to make amends. Perhaps she had sounded rather vengeful, there. 'I mean, yes, that's right,' she said, helping herself to milk but managing to slop most of it into the saucer.

Now the cup was going to drip all over everything. With an inward sigh, Cassie hunted around in her bag for a tissue to mop up the mess. 'I am.'

That sounded a bit too bald, didn't it? *You're supposed to be selling yourself here,* Cassie reminded herself, but she was distracted by the need to dispose of the sodden tissue now. She couldn't just leave it in the saucer. It looked disgusting, and so unprofessional.

'In the wedding business, that is,' she added, losing track

of where she had begun. Helplessly, she looked around for a bin, but of course there was nothing so prosaic in Jake's office.

It was immaculate, she noticed for the first time. Everything was squeaky clean, and the desk was clear except for a telephone and a very small, very expensive-looking computer. Ten years ago, Jake would only have been in an office like this to pinch the electronic equipment, she thought, wondering how on earth the rebel Jake, with his battered leathers and his bike, had made it to this exclusive, perfectly controlled space.

She could see Jake eyeing the tissue askance. Obviously any kind of mess offended him now, which was a shame, given that she was banking her entire future on being able to work closely with him and his fiancée for the next few months. Cassie belonged to the creative school of organising, the one that miraculously produced order out of chaos at the very last minute, although no one, least of all her, ever knew quite how it happened.

Unable to think of anything else do with it, Cassie quickly shoved the tissue back into her bag, where it would no doubt fester with all the other crumbs, chocolate wrappers, pen lids and blunt emery-boards that she never got round to clearing out. She would have to remember to be careful next time she put her hand in there.

Jake's expression was faintly disgusted, but he offered her the plate of biscuits. Cassie eyed them longingly. She was starving, but she knew better than to take one. The next thing, there would be biscuit crumbs everywhere, and her professional image had taken enough of a battering as it was this afternoon.

'No thank you,' she said politely, deciding to skip the coffee as well. At this rate she would just spill it all over herself and, worse, Jake's pristine leather sofa.

Leaning forward, Jake added milk to his own coffee without spilling so much as a drop. He stirred it briskly, tapped the spoon on the side of the cup, set it in the saucer and looked up at Cassie. The dark-blue eyes were very direct, and in spite of her determination to stay cool Cassie's pulse gave an alarming jolt.

'Well, shall we get down to business?' he suggested.

'Good idea.' Delighted to leave the past and all its embarrassing associations behind, Cassie leapt into action.

This was it. Her whole career—well, her job, Cassie amended to herself. She didn't have a career so much as a haphazard series of unrelated jobs. Anyway, *everything* depended on how she sold herself now.

Reaching for her briefcase, she unzipped it with a flourish, dug out a brochure and handed it to Jake. 'This will give you some idea of what we do,' she said in her best professional voice. It was odd that his fiancée wasn't here. Joss always aimed her pitch at the bride-to-be; she would just have to make the best of it, Cassie supposed.

'Of course, we offer a bespoke service, so we really start with what *you* want.' She hesitated. 'We usually discuss what you'd like with both members of the couple,' she added delicately. 'Will your fiancée be joining us?'

Jake had been flicking through the brochure, but at that he glanced up. 'Fiancée?'

'The bride generally has a good idea about what kind of wedding she wants,' Cassie explained. 'In our experience, grooms tend to be less concerned with the nitty-gritty of the organisation.'

'I think there may be some misunderstanding,' said Jake, frowning. 'I'm not engaged.'

Cassie's face fell ludicrously. 'Not…? You're not getting married?' she said, hoping against hope that she had misheard.

'No.'

Then how was she to hold on to her job? Cassie wondered wildly. 'So you don't need help planning a wedding?' she asked, just to make sure, and Jake let the brochure drop onto the table with a slap of finality.

'No.'

'But…' Cassie was struggling to understand how it could all have gone so wrong before she had even started. 'Why did you get in touch?'

'When Tina told me that you were in the wedding business I was under the impression that you managed a venue. I hadn't appreciated that you were involved with planning the weddings themselves.'

'Well, we *deal* with venues, of course,' said Cassie, desperate to hold on to something. 'We help couples with every aspect of the wedding and honeymoon.' She launched into her spiel, but Jake cut her off before she could really get going.

'I'm really looking for someone who can advise on what's involved in converting a house into a wedding venue. I'm sorry,' he said, making to get to his feet. 'It looks as if I've been wasting your time.'

Cassie wasn't ready to give up yet. 'We do that too,' she said quickly.

'What, waste time?'

'Set up wedding venues,' she said, refusing to rise to the bait, and meeting his eyes so guilelessly that Jake was fairly sure that she was lying. 'Between us, Joss and I have a lot of experience of using venues, and we know exactly what's required. Where is the house?' she asked quickly, before he could draw the conversation to a close.

'I'm thinking about the Hall,' he relented.

'The Hall?' Cassie repeated blankly. 'Portrevick Hall?'

'Exactly.'

'But…isn't it Rupert's now?'

'No,' said Jake. 'Sir Ian left the estate in trust and I'm the trustee.'

Cassie stared at him, her career crisis momentarily forgotten. '*You?*' she said incredulously.

He smiled grimly at her expression. 'Yes, me.'

'What about Rupert?' she asked, too surprised for tact.

'Sir Ian's money was left in trust for him. He hasn't proved the steadiest of characters, as you may know.'

Cassie did know. Rupert's picture was regularly in the gossip columns. There was a certain irony in the fact that Jake was now the wealthy, successful one while Rupert had a reputation as a hellraiser, albeit a very glamorous one. He seemed to get by largely on charm and those dazzling good looks.

She forced her attention back to Jake, who was still talking. 'Sir Ian was concerned that, if he left him the money outright, Rupert would just squander it the way he has already squandered his inheritance from his parents.'

'It just seems unfair,' she said tentatively. 'Rupert is Sir Ian's nephew, after all. I'm sure he expected to inherit Portrevick Hall.'

'I'm sure he did too,' said Jake in a dry voice. 'Rupert's been borrowing heavily on exactly that expectation for the last few years now. That's why Sir Ian put the estate into a trust. He was afraid Rupert would simply sell it off to the highest bidder otherwise.'

'But why make *you* the trustee?' said Cassie without thinking.

'It's not a position I angled for, I can assure you,' Jake said with a certain astringency. 'But I owe Sir Ian a lot, so I had to agree when he asked me. I assumed there would be plenty of time for him to change his mind, and he probably did the same. He was only in his sixties, and he'd had no history of heart problems. If only he'd lived longer…'

Restlessly, Jake pushed away his coffee cup and got to his feet. There was no point in 'if only's. 'Anyway, the fact remains that I'm stuck with responsibility for the house now. I promised Sir Ian that I would make sure the estate remained intact. He couldn't bear the thought of the Hall being broken up into flats, or holiday houses built in the grounds.

'Obviously, I need to fulfil his wishes, but I can't leave a house like that standing empty. It needs to be used and maintained, and somehow I've got to find a way for it to pay for itself.'

Coming to a halt by the window, Jake frowned unseeingly at the view while he remembered his problem. 'When I was down at Portrevick last week, sorting out things with the solicitor, she suggested that it might make a suitable wedding-venue. It seemed like an idea worth pursuing. I happened to mention it in the pub that night, and that's how your name came up. But, judging by your brochure, your company is more concerned with the weddings themselves rather than running the venues.'

'Normally, yes,' said Cassie, not so engrossed in the story of Sir Ian's extraordinary will that she had forgotten that her new-found career with Avalon was on the line. 'But the management of a venue is closely related to what we do, and in fact this is an area we're looking at moving into,' she added fluently. She would have to remember to tell Joss that they were diversifying. 'Clearly, we have considerable experience of dealing with various venues, so we're in a position to know exactly what facilities they need to offer.'

'Hmm.' Jake sounded unconvinced. He turned from the window to study Cassie, sitting alert and eager on the sofa. 'All right, you know the Hall. Given your *considerable experience*, what would you think of it as a wedding venue?'

'It would be perfect,' said Cassie, ignoring his sarcasm. 'It's a beautiful old house with a wonderful location on the coast. It would be hard to imagine anywhere more romantic! I should think couples all over the South West would be queuing up to get married there.'

Jake came back to sit opposite her once more. He drummed his fingers absently on the table, obviously thinking. 'It's encouraging that you think it would make a popular venue, anyway,' he said at last.

'Yes, I do,' said Cassie eagerly, sensing that Jake might be buying her spur-of-the-moment career shift into project management.

She leant forward persuasively. 'I'm sure Sir Ian would

approve of the idea,' she went on. 'He loved people, didn't he? I bet he would have liked to see the Hall used for weddings. They're such happy occasions.'

'If you say so,' said Jake, clearly unconvinced.

He studied Cassie with a faint frown, wondering if he was mad to even consider taking her advice. She had always been a dreamer, he remembered, and the curly hair and dimple gave her a warm, sweet but slightly dishevelled air that completely contradicted the businesslike suit and the stylish, totally impractical shoes.

There was something chaotic about Cassie, Jake decided. Even sitting still, she gave the alarming impression that she was on the verge of knocking something over or making a mess. Good grief, the girl couldn't even manage walking into a room without falling over her own shoes! Having spent the last few years cultivating a careful sense of order and control, Jake found the aura of unpredictability Cassie exuded faintly disturbing.

He had a strong suspicion, too, that Cassie's experience of managing a venue was no wider than his own. She was clearly desperate for work, and would say whatever she thought he wanted to hear.

If he had any sense, he would close the meeting right now.

CHAPTER TWO

ON THE other hand...

On the other hand, Jake reminded himself, Sir Ian had been fond of her, and the fact that she knew the Hall was an undoubted advantage.

He could at least give her the chance to convince him that she knew what she was talking about. For old times' sake, thought Jake, looking at Cassie's mouth.

'So what would need to be done to make the Hall a venue?' he asked abruptly. 'Presumably we'd have to get a licence?'

'Absolutely,' said Cassie with more confidence than she was feeling. 'I imagine it would need quite a bit of refurbishment, too. You can charge a substantial fee for the hire of the venue, but in return couples will expect everything to be perfect. All the major rooms would have to be completely redecorated, and anything shabby or dingy replaced.'

Cassie was making it up as she went along, but she was banking on the fact that Jake knew less than she did about what weddings involved. Besides, how difficult could it be? She couldn't let a little thing like not knowing what she was talking about stop her, not when the alternative was losing her job and having to admit to her family that she had failed again.

'Naturally you would have to set it up so that everything is laid on,' she went on, rather enjoying the authoritative note in her own voice. She would convince *herself* at this rate! 'You need to think about catering, flowers, music; whatever a bride and groom could possibly want. They're paying a lot of money for their big day, so you've got to make it very special for them.

'Some people like to make all the arrangements them-selves,' she told Jake, who was listening with a kind of hor-rified fascination. 'But if you want the Hall to be successful you'll have to make it possible for them to hand over all the arrangements to the staff and not think about anything. That means being prepared to cater for every whim, as well as dif-ferent kinds of weddings. It might just be a reception, or it might be the wedding itself, and that could include all sorts of different faiths, as well as civil partnerships.'

Cassie was really getting into her stride now. 'Then you need to think about what other facilities you're going to provide,' she said, impressing herself with her own fluency. Who would have thought she could come out with this stuff off the top of her head? All those weddings she had attended over the past few months must have paid off.

'The bride and groom will want somewhere to change, at the very least, or they might want to take over the whole house for a wedding party. You'll need new kitchens too. Loos, obviously. And, of course, you'll have to think about finding staff and making contacts with local caterers, florists, photographers and so on.

'There's marketing and publicity to consider as well,' she pointed out. 'Eventually, you'll be able to rely on word of mouth, but it'll be important until you're established.'

Jake was looking appalled. 'I didn't realise it was such a business,' he admitted. 'You mean it's not enough to clear the great hall for dancing and lay on a few white tablecloths?'

'I'm afraid not.'

There was a long pause. Jake's mouth was turned down, and Cassie could see him rethinking the whole idea.

Oh God, what if she had put him off? She bit her lip. That was what you got for showing off.

You always go a bit too far. How many times when she had been growing up had her mother said that to her? Cassie could practically hear her saying it now.

Anxiously, she watched Jake's face. It was impossible to tell what he was thinking.

'We're talking about a substantial investment,' he said slowly at last, and Cassie let out a long breath she hadn't known she was holding.

'Yes, but it'll be worth it,' she said, trying to disguise her relief. 'Weddings are big business. If you aim for the top end of the market, the house will more than pay for itself.'

Jake was still not entirely convinced. 'It's a lot to think about.'

'Not if you let us oversee everything for you,' said Cassie, marvelling at her own nerve. 'We could manage the whole project and set it up until it's ready to hand over to a permanent manager.'

It was a brilliant idea, even if she said so herself. She couldn't think why Joss hadn't thought of going into venue management before.

Jake was watching her with an indecipherable expression. Cassie lifted her chin and tried to look confident, half-expecting him to accuse her—accurately—of bluffing, but in the end he just asked how they structured their fees.

'I'd have to discuss that with Joss when we've got a clearer idea of exactly what needs to be done,' said Cassie evasively. Joss was much harder-headed when it came to money and always dealt with the financial side of things.

'OK.' Jake made up his mind abruptly. 'Let me have a detailed proposal and I'll consider it.'

'Great.' Cassie's relief was rapidly being overtaken by panic. What on earth had she committed herself to?

'So, what next?'

Yes, what next, Cassie? Cassie gulped. 'I think I need to take another look at the Hall and draw up a list of work required,' she improvised.

Fortunately, this seemed to be the right thing to say. Jake nodded. 'That makes sense. Can you come to Cornwall on Thursday? I've got to go back myself to see the solicitor, so we could drive down together if that suits you.'

It didn't, but Cassie knew better than to say so. Having bluffed this far, she couldn't give up now. A seven-hour car journey with Jake Trevelyan wasn't her idea of a fun day, but if she could pull off a contract it would be worth it.

'Of course,' she said, relaxing enough to pick up her coffee at last, and promptly splashing it over her skirt. She brushed the drops away hastily, hoping that Jake hadn't noticed. 'I can be ready to leave whenever you are.'

Jake watched Cassie practically fall out of the door, struggling with a weekend case on wheels, a motley collection of plastic carrier-bags and a handbag that kept slipping down her arm. With a sigh, he got out of the car to help her. He was double parked outside her office, and had hoped for a quick getaway, but clearly that wasn't going to happen.

He hadn't made many mistakes in the last ten years, but Jake had a nasty feeling that appointing Cassie to manage the transformation of Portrevick Hall into a wedding venue might be one of them. He had been secretly impressed by the fluent way she had talked about weddings, and by the way she had seemed to know exactly what was involved, but at the same time her lack of experience was obvious. And yet she had fixed him with those big, brown eyes and distracted him with that mouth, and before Jake had quite known what he was doing he had agreed to give her the job.

He must have been mad, he decided as he took the case from her. Cassie had to be the least organised organiser he had ever met. *Look at her*, laden with carrier bags, the wayward brown curls blowing around face, her cardigan all twisted under the weight of her handbag!

She was a mess, Jake thought disapprovingly. She was

casually dressed in a mishmash of colourful garments that appeared to be thrown together without any thought for neatness or elegance. Yes, she had grown into a surprisingly pretty girl, but she could do with some of Natasha's poise and sophistication.

He stashed the carrier bags in the boot with the case. 'What on earth do you need all this stuff for?' he demanded. 'We're only going for a couple of nights.'

'Most of it's Tina's. She came to London months ago and left half her clothes behind, so I'm taking them back to her. She's invited me to stay with her,' Cassie added.

Jake was sleeping at the Hall, and he'd suggested that Cassie stay there as well, but Cassie couldn't help thinking it all seemed a bit intimate. True, the Hall had bedrooms to spare, but they would still be sleeping in the same place, bumping into each other on the way to the bathroom, wandering into the kitchen in their PJs to make tea in the morning... No; Cassie wasn't ready to meet Jake without her make-up on yet.

'I thought I might as well stay for the weekend, since I'm down there,' she went on, talking over the roof of the car as she made her way round to the passenger door. 'I haven't seen Tina for ages. I might talk to some local contractors on Monday, too, and then come back on the train.'

Cassie knew that she was talking too much, but the prospect of the long journey in Jake's company was making her stupidly jittery. She had been fine until he'd appeared. Joss had given her unqualified approval to the plan, and Cassie had been enjoying dizzying fantasies about her new career in project management.

It had been a strange experience, seeing Jake again, and she'd been left disorientated by the way he looked familiar but behaved like a total stranger. In some ways, that made it easier to dissassociate him from the Jake she had known in the past. This Jake was less menacing than the old one, for sure. The surliness and resentment had been replaced by steely control, but it was somehow just as intimidating.

But at least she had the possibility of a job, Cassie reminded herself sternly as she got into the car. She had to concentrate on that, and not on the unnerving prospect of being shut up in a car with Jake Trevelyan. He had come straight from his office and was still wearing his suit, but, having slammed the boot shut, he took off his jacket, loosened his tie and rolled up his shirt sleeves before getting back into the driver's seat.

'Right,' he said briskly, switching on the ignition. 'Let's go.'

It was a big, luxuriously comfortable car with swish leather seats, but Cassie felt cramped and uneasy as she pulled on the seatbelt. It wouldn't have been so bad if Jake wasn't just *there*, only inches away, filling the whole car with his dark, forceful presence, using up all the available oxygen so that she had to open the window to drag in a breath.

'There's air conditioning,' said Jake, using the electric controls on his side to close it again.

Air conditioning. Right. So how come it was so hard to breathe?

'I was half-expecting you to turn up on a motorbike,' she said chattily, to conceal her nervousness.

'It's just as well I didn't, with all those bags you've brought along with you.' Jake checked his mirror, indicated and pulled out into the traffic.

'I always fancied the idea of riding pillion,' said Cassie.

'I don't think you'd fancy it all the way down to Cornwall,' Jake said, dampening her. 'You'll be much more comfortable in a car.'

Under normal circumstances, maybe, but Cassie couldn't imagine anything less comfortable than being shut up with him in a confined space for seven hours. They had barely left Fulham, but the car seemed to have shrunk already, and she was desperately aware of Jake beside her. Her eyes kept snagging on his hands, strong and competent on the steering wheel, and she would find herself remembering how they had felt on her arms as he had yanked her towards him.

Turning her head to remove them from her vision, Cassie found herself looking awkwardly out of the side window, but that was hard on her neck. Before she knew it, her eyes were skittering back to Jake's side of the car, to the line of his cheek, the corner of his mouth and the faint prickle of stubble under his jaw where he had wrenched impatiently at his tie to loosen it.

She could see the pulse beating steadily in his throat, and for one bizarre moment let herself imagine what it would be like to lean across and press her lips to it. Then she imagined Jake jerking away in horror and losing control of the car, which would crash into that newsagent's, and then the police would come and she would have to make a statement: *I'm sorry, officer, I was just overcome by an uncontrollable urge to kiss Jake Trevelyan.*

It would be in all the papers, and in no time at all the news would reach the Portrevick Arms, where they would all snigger. Village memories were long. No one would have forgotten what a fool she had made of herself over Rupert, and they would shake their heads and tell each other that Cassandra Grey never had been able to keep her hands off a man...

Cassie's heart was thumping just at the thought of it, and she jerked her head back to the side, ignoring the protest of her neck muscles.

Comfortable? Hah!

'Besides,' Jake went on as Cassie offered up thanks that he hadn't spent the last ten years learning to read minds, 'I haven't got a motorbike any more. I've left my biking days behind me.'

It would have been impossible to imagine Jake without that mean-looking bike years ago in Portrevick.

'You've changed,' said Cassie.

'I sincerely hope so,' said Jake.

Why couldn't she have changed that much? Cassie wondered enviously. If she had, she could be svelte and sophisticated, with a successful career behind her, instead of muddling along feeling most of the time much as she had at seventeen. She might look different, but deep down she felt just the same as she had done then. How had Jake done it?

'What have you been doing for the past ten years?' she asked him curiously.

'I've been in the States for most of them. I got myself a degree, and then did an MBA at Harvard.'

'*Really?*' said Cassie, impressed. In all the years she had wondered where Jake Trevelyan was and what he was doing, she had never considered that he might be at university. She had imagined him surfing, perhaps, or running a bar on some beach somewhere, or possibly making shady deals astride his motorbike—but *Harvard*? Even her father would be impressed by that.

'I had no idea,' she said.

Jake shrugged. 'I was lucky. I went to work for a smallish firm in Seattle, just as it was poised for expansion. It was an exciting time, and it gave me a lot of valuable experience. That company was at the forefront of digital technology, and Primordia is in the same field, which put me in a good position when they were looking for a new Chief Executive, although it took some negotiation to get me back to London.'

'Didn't you want to come back?'

'Not particularly. But they made me an offer even I couldn't refuse.'

'You were head-hunted?' said Cassie, trying to imagine a company going out of its way to recruit her. *Cassandra Grey's just the person we want for this job*, they would say. *How can we tempt her?*

Nope, she couldn't do it.

Jake obviously took the whole business for granted. 'That's how it works.' He pulled up at a red light and glanced at Cassie. 'What about you? How long have you been with Avalon?'

'Just since the beginning of the year. Before that I was a receptionist,' she said. 'I did a couple of stints in retail, a bit of temping, a bit of waitressing...'

She sighed. 'Not a very impressive career, as my father is always pointing out. I'm a huge disappointment to my parents. The others have all done really well. They all went to Cambridge. Liz is a doctor, Tom's an architect and even Jack is a lawyer now. They're all grown-ups, and I'm just the family problem.'

Cassie had intended the words to sound humorous, but was uneasily aware they had come out rather flat. Rather as if she didn't think it was such a funny joke after all. 'They're always ringing each other up and wondering what to do about Cassie.'

But that was all going to change, she reminded herself. This could be the start of a whole new career. She was going to turn Portrevick Hall into a model venue. Celebrities would be queuing up to get married there. After a year or two, they wouldn't even have to advertise. Just mentioning that a wedding would be at Portrevick Hall would mean that it would be the last word in style and elegance.

Cassandra Grey? they would say. *Isn't she the one who made Portrevick Hall a byword for chic and exclusive?* She would get tired of calls from the head-hunters. *Not again*, she would sigh. *When are you people going to get the message that I don't want to commit to one job?* Because, of course, by then she would be a consultant. She had always fancied the thought of being one of those.

Cassie settled herself more comfortably in her seat, liking the way this fantasy was going. All those smart hotels in London would be constantly ringing her up and begging her to come and sort out their events facilities—and probably not just in London, now she came to think of it. She would have an international reputation.

Yes, she'd get tired of jetting off to New York and Dubai and Sydney. Cassie smiled to herself. Liz, Tom and Jack would still be ringing each other up, but instead of worrying about her they would be complaining about how humdrum their sensible careers seemed in comparison with her glamorous life. *I'm sick of Cassie telling me she'd really just like a few days at home doing nothing*, Liz would grumble.

'And what's Cassie going to do about herself?' asked Jake, breaking rudely into her dream.

'I'm going to do what I'm doing,' she told him firmly. 'I love working for Joss at Avalon. It's the best job I've ever had, and I'll do anything to keep it.'

Even pretending to understand about project management, she added mentally.

'What does a wedding planner *do* all day?'

'It could be anything,' she said. 'I might book string quartets, or find exactly the right shade of ribbon, or source an unusual cake-topper. I love the variety. I can be helping a bride to choose her dress one minute, and sorting out accommodation for the wedding party the next. And then, of course, I get to go to all the weddings.'

Jake made a face. He couldn't think of anything worse. 'It sounds hellish,' he said frankly. 'Don't you get bored?'

'Never,' said Cassie. 'I love weddings. I cry every time— I do!' she insisted when he looked at her in disbelief.

'Why? These people are clients, not friends.'

'They feel like friends by the time we've spent months together planning the wedding,' she retorted. 'But it doesn't matter whether I know the bride and groom or not. I always want to cry when I walk past Chelsea register office and see people on the steps after they've got married. I love seeing everyone so happy. A wedding is such a *hopeful* occasion.'

'In spite of all the evidence to the contrary,' said Jake astringently. 'How many of those weddings you're snivelling at this year will end in divorce by the end of the next? Talk about the triumph of hope over experience!'

'But that's exactly why weddings are so moving,' said

Cassie. 'They're about people choosing to love each other. Lots of people get married more than once. They know how difficult marriage can be, but they still want to make that commitment. I think it's wonderful,' she added defiantly. 'What have you got against marriage, anyway?'

'I've got nothing against marriage,' said Jake. 'It's all the expense and fuss of weddings that I find pointless. It seems to me that marriage is a serious business, and you should approach it in a serious way, not muddle it all up with big dresses, flowers, cakes and whatever else goes on at weddings these days.'

'Weddings are meant to be a celebration,' she reminded him. 'What do you want the bride and groom to do instead— sit down and complete a checklist?'

'At least then they would know they were compatible.'

Cassie rolled her eyes. 'So what would be on your checklist?'

'I'd want to know that the woman I was marrying was intelligent, and sensible...and confident,' Jake decided. 'More importantly, I'd need to be sure that we shared the same goals, that we both had the same attitude to success in our careers... and sex, of course...and to little things like tidiness that can put the kybosh on a relationship quicker than anything else.'

'You don't ask for much, do you?' said Cassie tartly, reflecting that she wouldn't get many ticks on Jake's checklist. In fact, if he had set out to describe her exact opposite, he could hardly have done a better job. 'Clever, confident, successful and tidy. Where are you going to find a paragon like that?'

'I already have,' said Jake.

Oh.

'Oh,' said Cassie, unaccountably put out. 'What's her name?'

'Natasha. We've been together six months.'

'So why haven't you married her if she's so perfect?' Try as she might, Cassie couldn't keep the snippiness from her voice.

'We just haven't got round to talking about it,' said Jake. 'I think it would be a good move, though. It makes sense.'

'Makes sense?' echoed Cassie in disbelief. 'You should get married because you're in love, not because it *makes sense*!'

'In my book, committing yourself to someone for life because you're in love is what *doesn't* make sense,' he retorted.

Crikey, whatever happened to romance? Cassie shook her head. 'Well, if you ever decide that doing a checklist together isn't quite enough, remember that Avalon can help you plan your wedding.'

'I'll bear it in mind,' he said. 'I imagine Natasha would like a wedding of some kind, but she's a very successful solicitor, so she wouldn't have the time to organise much herself.'

Of course, Natasha *would* be a successful solicitor, Cassie thought, having taken a dislike to his perfect girlfriend without ever having met her. She was tempted to say that Natasha would no doubt be too busy being marvellous to have time to bother with anything as inconsequential as a wedding, but remembered in time that Avalon's business relied on brides being too busy to do everything themselves.

Besides, it might sound as if she was jealous of Natasha. Which was nonsense, of course.

'I certainly wouldn't know where to start,' Jake went on. 'Weddings are unfamiliar territory to me.'

'You must have been to loads of weddings, mustn't you?'

'Very few,' he said. 'In fact, only a couple. I lived in the States until last year, so I missed out on various family weddings.'

'I don't know how you managed to avoid them,' said Cassie. 'All my friends seem have got married in the last year or so. There was a time when it felt as if I was going to a wedding every other weekend, and that was just people I knew! It was as if it was catching. Suddenly everyone was married.'

'Everyone except you?'

'That's what it feels like, anyway,' she said with little sigh.

'Why not you? You're obviously not averse to the idea of getting married.'

'I just haven't found the right guy, I suppose.' Cassie sighed again. 'I've had boyfriends, of course, but none of them have had that special something.'

Jake slanted a sardonic glance at her. 'Don't tell me you're still holding out for Rupert Branscombe Fox?'

'Of course not,' she said, flushing with embarrassment at the memory of the massive crush she had had on Rupert.

Not that she could really blame herself. What seventeen-year-old girl could be expected to resist that lethal combination of good looks and glamour? And Rupert could be extraordinarily charming when he wanted to be. He wasn't so charming when he didn't, of course, as Cassie had discovered even before Jake had kissed her.

Whoops; she didn't want to be thinking about that kiss, did she?

Too late.

Cassie tried the looking-out-of-the window thing again, but London was a blur, and she was back outside the Hall again, being yanked against Jake again. She could smell the leather of his jacket, feel the hardness of his body and the unforgiving steel of the motorbike.

In spite of Cassie's increasingly desperate efforts to keep her eyes on the interminable houses lining the road, they kept sliding round to Jake's profile. The traffic was heavy and he was concentrating on driving, so she gave in and let them skitter over the angular planes of his face to the corner of his mouth, at which point her heart started thumping and thudding alarmingly.

It was ten years later. Jake had changed completely. The leather jacket had gone, the bike had gone.

But that mouth was still exactly the same.

That mouth... She knew what it felt like. She knew how it tasted. She knew just how warm and sure those firm lips could be. Jake was an austere stranger beside her now, but she had *kissed* him. The memory was so vivid and so disorientating that Cassie felt quite giddy for a moment.

She swallowed. 'I had a major crush on Rupert, but it was just a teenage thing. Remember what a gawk I was?' she said, removing her gaze firmly back to the road. 'I have this fantasy that if I bumped into Rupert now he wouldn't recognise me.'

'I recognised you,' Jake pointed out unhelpfully.

'Yes, well, that's the thing about fantasies,' Cassie retorted in a tart voice. 'They're not real. I'm never likely to meet Rupert again. He lives in a different world, and the closest I get to him is seeing his picture in a celebrity magazine with some incredibly beautiful woman on his arm. Even if by some remote chance I did meet him I know he wouldn't even *notice* me, let along recognise me.'

'Why not?'

'Oh, I'm much too ordinary for the likes of Rupert,' said Cassie with a sigh. 'You were right about that, anyway.'

Jake looked taken aback. 'When did I ever say you were ordinary?'

'You know when.' She flashed him an accusing glance. 'After the Allentide Ball.' *After you kissed me.* 'Before you punched Rupert on the nose. I gather you took it upon yourself to tell Rupert I wasn't nearly sophisticated enough for him.'

It still rankled after all these years.

'You weren't,' said Jake.

'Then why were you fighting?'

'Not because Rupert leapt to defend your sophistication and readiness to embark on a torrid affair, if that's what you were thinking!'

'He said you'd been offensive,' said Cassie.

'Did he?' said Jake with a certain grimness.

It was typical of Rupert to have twisted the truth, he thought. He had been sitting at the bar, having a quiet drink, when Rupert had strolled in with his usual tame audience. Jake had found Rupert's arrogance difficult to deal with at the best of times, and that night certainly hadn't been one of those.

Jake often wondered how his life would have turned out if

he hadn't been in a particularly bad temper that night. The raw, piercing sweetness of Cassie's kiss at the Allentide ball had caught him unawares, and it didn't help that she had so patently been using him to attract Rupert's attention. Jake had been left feeling edgy, and furious with himself for expecting that it could have been any different and caring one way or the other.

And then Rupert had been there, showing off as usual. He'd been boasting about having had the estate manager's ungainly daughter, and making the others laugh. Jake's hand had clenched around his glass. He might not have liked being used, but Cassie was very young. She hadn't deserved to have her first experience of sex made the subject of pub banter.

Rupert had gone on and on, enjoying his audience, and Jake had finally had enough. He'd set down his glass very deliberately and risen to his feet to face Rupert. There had been a chorus of taunting, 'Ooohs' when he'd told him to leave Cassie alone, but he'd at least had the satisfaction of wiping the smirks off all their faces.

Especially Rupert's. Jake smiled ferociously as he remembered how he had released years of pent-up resentment. The moment his fist had connected with Rupert's nose had been a sweet one, and worth being banned from the village pub for. If it hadn't been for that fight, Rupert wouldn't have talked about assault charges, news of the fight wouldn't have reached Sir Ian's ears, and he wouldn't be where he was now.

Oh yes; it had definitely been worth it.

CHAPTER THREE

'IT's my word against Rupert's, I suppose, but I can tell you, I was never offensive about you,' he said to Cassie. 'And being ordinary isn't the same thing as not being sophisticated. Believe me, you've never struck me as ordinary!'

'But I am,' said Cassie glumly. 'Or I am compared to Rupert, anyway. He's just so glamorous. Even you'd have to admit that.'

Jake's snort suggested he wasn't prepared to admit anything of the kind.

Of course, he'd never had any time for Rupert. Cassie supposed she could understand it. Rupert might be handsome, but even at the height of her crush she had recognised that arrogance in him as well. At the time, she had thought that it just added to his air of glamour.

The truth was that she still had a soft spot for Rupert, so good-looking and so badly behaved. In another age, he would have been a rake, ravishing women left, right and centre. Cassie could just see him in breeches and ruffles, smiling that irresistible smile, and breaking hearts without a flicker of shame.

Not the kind of man you would want to marry, perhaps, but very attractive all the same.

Cassie sighed a little wistfully. 'Rupert could be very charming,' she tried to explain, not that Jake was likely to be convinced.

They had barely got going on the motorway, and already overhead gantries were flashing messages about queues ahead. Muttering in frustration, he eased his foot up from the accelerator.

'What's so charming about squandering an inheritance from your parents and then sponging off your uncle?' he demanded irritably. 'Sir Ian got tired of bailing him out in the end, but he did what he could to encourage Rupert to settle down. He left his fortune to Rupert in trust until he's forty, in the hope that by then he'll have come to his senses.'

'Forty?' Cassie gasped. Rupert was only in his early thirties, like Jake, and eight years would be an eternity to wait when you had a lifestyle like Rupert's. 'That's awful,' she said without thinking. 'What's he going to do?'

'He could always try getting a job like the rest of us,' said Jake astringently 'Or, if he really can't bring himself to do anything as sordid as earning his own living, he can always get married. Sir Ian specified that the trust money could be released if Rupert gets married and settles down. He can't just marry anyone to get his hands on the money, though. He'll have to convince me as trustee that it's a real marriage and his wife a sensible woman before I'll release the funds.'

'Gosh, Rupert must have been livid when he found out!'

'He wasn't too happy,' Jake agreed with masterly understatement. 'He tried to contest the will, and when he didn't get anywhere with that he suggested we try and discuss things in a "civilised" way—which I gather meant me ignoring Sir Ian's wishes and handing the estate over to him to do with as he pleased.

'I was prepared to be civilised, of course. I invited him round for a drink, and it was just like old times,' he went on ironically. 'Rupert was arrogant and patronising, and I wanted to break his nose again!'

'You didn't!'

'No,' admitted Jake. 'But I don't know what would have happened if Natasha hadn't been there.'

'What did she make of Rupert?'

'She thought he was shallow.'

'I bet she thought he was gorgeous too,' said Cassie with a provocative look, and Jake pokered up and looked down his nose.

'Natasha is much too sensible to judge people on their appearances,' he said stiffly.

Of course she was. Cassie rolled her eyes as they overtook a van that was hogging the middle lane, startling the driver, who gave a grimace that was well out of Jake's field of vision. The van moved smartly into the slow lane.

'So how come she got involved with you if she's so sensible?' she asked, forgetting for a moment that Jake was an important client.

'We get on very well,' said Jake austerely.

'What does getting on very well mean, exactly?'

Ahead, there was a flurry of red lights as cars braked, and Jake moved smoothly into the middle lane. 'It means we're very compatible,' he said.

And they were. Natasha was everything he admired in a woman. She was very attractive—beautiful, in fact—and clear-thinking. She didn't constantly demand emotional reassurance the way his previous girlfriends had. She was focused on her own career, and understood if he had to work late, as he often did. She never made a fuss.

And she was classy. That was a large part of her appeal, Jake was prepared to admit. Years ago in Portrevick, Natasha wouldn't have looked at him twice, but when he walked into a party with her on his arm now he knew that he had arrived. She was everything Jake had never known when he was growing up. She had the assurance that came from a life of wealth and privilege, and every time Jake looked at her she reassured him that he had left Portrevick and the past behind him at last.

He didn't feel like telling Cassie all of that, though.

The traffic had slowed to a crawl and Jake shifted gear. 'I hope this is just sheer weight of traffic,' he said. 'I don't want to spend any more time on the road than we have to.'

Nor did Cassie. She wriggled in her seat. Quite apart from anything else, she was starving. Afraid that she would be late, she hadn't had time for breakfast that morning, and her stomach was gurgling ominously. She was hoping Jake would stop for petrol at some point, but at this rate they'd be lucky to get to a service station for supper, let alone lunch.

The lines of cars were inching forward in a staggered pattern. Sometimes the lane on their left would have a spurt of movement, only to grind to a halt as the supposed fast-lane speeded up, and then it would be the middle lane's turn. They kept passing or being passed by the same cars, and Cassie was beginning to recognise the occupants.

An expensive saloon on their left was creeping ahead of them once more. Covertly, Cassie studied the driver and passenger, both of whom were staring grimly ahead and not talking.

'I bet they've had a row,' she said.

'Who?'

'The couple on our left in the blue car.' Cassie pointed discreetly. 'Have a look when we go past. I can't decide whether she left the top off the toothpaste again, or whether she's incredibly possessive and sulking because he just had a text from his secretary.'

Jake cast her an incredulous glance. 'What's wrong with getting a text from your secretary?'

'She thinks he's having an affair with her,' said Cassie, barely pausing to consider. 'She insists on answering his phone while he's driving. Of course the text was completely bland, just confirming some meeting or something, but she just *knows* that it's a code.'

It was their lane's turn to move. Against his better judgement, Jake found himself glancing left as they passed. Cassie was right; the people both looked hatched-faced.

'They could be going to visit the in-laws,' he suggested, drawn into the fantasy in spite of himself.

Cassie took another look. 'You might be right,' she allowed. 'Her parents?'

'His, I think. She's got a face like concrete, so she's doing something she doesn't want to do. They don't really approve of her.'

'Hey, you're good at this!' Cassie laughed and swivelled back to watch the traffic. 'Now, who have we got here?' They were passing a hatchback driven by an elderly man who was clutching onto the wheel for dear life. Beside him, a tiny old lady was talking. 'Grandparents off to visit their daughter,' she said instantly. 'Too easy.'

'Perhaps they've been having a wild affair and are running away together,' said Jake, tongue in cheek.

'I like the way you're thinking, but they look way too comfortable together for that. I bet she's been talking for hours and he hasn't heard a word.'

'Can't imagine what that feels like,' murmured Jake, and she shot him a look.

'I wonder what they think about us?' she mused.

'I doubt very much that anyone else is thinking about us at all.'

'We must look like any other couple heading out of town for a long weekend,' said Cassie, ignoring him.

Perhaps that was why it felt so intimate sitting here beside him. If they were a couple, she could rest her hand on Jake's thigh. She could unwrap a toffee and pop it in his mouth without thinking. She could put her feet up on the dashboard and choose some music, and they could argue about which was the best route. She could nag him about stopping for something to eat.

But of course she couldn't do any of that. Especially not laying a hand on his leg.

She turned her attention firmly back to the other cars.

'Ooh, now…' she said, spying a single middle-aged man looking harassed at the wheel of his car, and instantly wove a complicated story about the double life he was leading, naming both wives, all five children and even the hamster with barely a pause for breath.

Jake shook his head. He tried to imagine Natasha speculating about the occupants of the other cars, and couldn't do it. She would think it childish. As it was, thought Jake.

On the other hand, this traffic jam was a lot less tedious than others he had sat in. Cassie's expression was animated, and he was very aware of her beside him. She had pushed back the seat as far as it would go, and her legs, in vivid blue tights, were stretched out before her. Her mobile face was alight with humour, her hands in constant motion. Jake had a jumbled impression of colour and warmth tugging at the edges of his vision the whole time. It was very distracting.

Now she was pulling faces at a little boy in the back seat of the car beside them. He crossed his eyes and stuck out his tongue, while Cassie stuck her thumbs in her ears and waggled her fingers in response.

Jake was torn between exasperation and amusement. He didn't know where Cassie got her idea that she was ordinary. There was absolutely nothing ordinary about her that he could see.

He glanced at the clock as they inched forward. It was a bad sign that they were hitting heavy traffic this early. It wasn't even midday, and already they seemed to have been travelling for ever.

Cassie had fallen silent at last. Bizarrely, Jake almost missed her ridiculous stories. Suddenly there was a curdled growl that startled him out of his distraction. He glanced at Cassie in surprise and she blushed and folded her arms over her stomach.

'Sorry, that was me,' she apologised. 'I didn't have time for breakfast.'

How embarrassing! Cassie was mortified. Natasha's stomach would never even murmur. At least Jake seemed prepared to cope with the problem.

'We'll stop and get something to eat when we get out of this,' he promised, but it was another twenty minutes before the blockage cleared, miraculously and for no apparent reason, and he could put his foot down.

To Cassie's disappointment they didn't stop at the first service-station they came to, or even the second. 'We need to get as far on our way as we can,' Jake said, but as her stomach became increasingly vocal he eventually relented as they came up to the third.

After a drizzly summer, the sun had finally come out for September. 'Let's sit outside,' Cassie suggested when they had bought coffee and sandwiches. 'We should make the most of the sun while we've got it.'

They found a wooden table in a sunny spot, away from the ceaseless growl of the motorway. Cassie turned sideways so that she could straddle the bench, and turned her face up to the sun.

'I love September,' she said. 'It still feels like the start of a new school year. I want to sharpen my pencils and write my name at the front of a blank exercise-book.'

Perhaps that was why she was so excited about transforming Portrevick Hall into a wedding venue, Cassie thought as she unwrapped her sandwich. It was a whole new project, her chance to draw a line under all her past muddles and mistakes and start afresh. She was determined not to mess up this time.

'It's great to get out of London too,' she went on indistinctly through a mouthful of egg mayonnaise. 'I'm really looking forward to seeing Portrevick again, too. I haven't been back since my parents moved away, but the place where you grow up always feels like home, doesn't it?'

'No,' said Jake.

'Really?' Cassie was brushing egg from her skirt, but at that she looked up at him in surprise. 'Don't you miss it at all?'

'I miss the sea sometimes,' he said after a moment. 'But Portrevick? No. It's not such a romantic place to live when there's never any money, and the moment there's trouble the police are at your door wanting you to account for where you've been and what you've been doing.'

Jake could hear the bitterness seeping into his voice in spite of every effort to keep it neutral. Cassie had no idea. She had grown up in a solid, cosy house in a solid, cosy, middle-class family. They might have lived in the same place, but they had inhabited different worlds.

Miss it? He had spent ten years trying to put Portrevick behind him.

'You must have family still there, though, mustn't you?' said Cassie. There had always been lots of Trevelyans in Portrevick, all of them reputedly skirting around the edges of the law.

'Not in Portrevick,' said Jake. 'There's no work in a village like that any more.' And there were richer pickings in places like Newquay or Penzance, he thought dryly. 'They've all moved away, so there's no one to go back for. If it wasn't for Sir Ian and the trust, I'd be happy never to see Portrevick again. And once I've sorted out something for the Hall I'll be leaving and I won't ever be going back.'

Cassie was having trouble keeping the filling in her sandwich. The egg kept oozing out of the baguette and dropping everywhere. Why hadn't she chosen a nice, neat sandwich like Jake's ham and cheese? He was managing to eat his without any mess at all.

She eyed him under her lashes as she licked her finger and gathered up some of the crumbs that were scattered on her side of the table. Jake had always been such a cool figure in her memories of Portrevick that it had never occurred to her to wonder how happy he had been.

He hadn't seemed unhappy. In Cassie's mind, he had always flirted with danger, roaring around on his motorbike or surfing in the roughest seas. She could still see him, sleek and dark as a seal in his wetsuit, riding the surf, his body leaning and bending in tune with the rolling wave.

It was hard to believe it was the same man as the one who sat across the table from her now, contained and controlled, eating his sandwich methodically. What had happened to that fierce, reckless boy?

Abandoning her sandwich for a moment, Cassie took a sip of coffee. 'If you feel like that about Portrevick, why did you agree to be Sir Ian's trustee?'

'Because I owed him.'

Jake had finished his own sandwich and brushed the crumbs from his fingers. 'It was Sir Ian that got me out of Portrevick,' he told her. 'He was always good to my mother, and after she died he let me earn some money by doing odd jobs for him. He was from a different world, but I liked him. He was the only person in the village who'd talk to you as if he was really interested in what you had to say. I was just a difficult kid from a problem family, but I never once had the feeling that Sir Ian was looking down on me.'

Unlike his nephew, Jake added to himself. Rupert got up every morning, looked in the mirror and found himself perfect. From the dizzying heights of his pedestal, how could he do anything *but* look down on lesser mortals? A boy from a dubious family and without the benefit of private schooling… Well, clearly Jake ought to be grateful that Rupert had ever noticed him at all.

'Sir Ian was lovely,' Cassie was agreeing. 'I know he was a bit eccentric, but he always made you feel that you were the one person he really wanted to see.'

Jake nodded. He had felt that, too. 'I saw him the day after that fight with Rupert,' he went on. 'Rupert was all set to press assault charges against me, but Sir Ian said he would persuade him to drop them. In return, he told me I should leave Portrevick. He said that if I stayed I would never shake off my family's reputation. There would be other fights, other brushes with the police. I'd drift over the line the way my father had done and end up in prison.'

Turning the beaker between his hands, Jake looked broodingly down into his coffee, remembering the conversation. Sir Ian hadn't pulled his punches. 'You're a bright lad,' he had said. 'But you're in danger of wasting all the potential you've got. You're eaten up with resentment, you're a troublemaker and you take stupid risks. If you're not careful, you'll end up in prison too. You can make a new life for yourself if you want it, but you're going to have to work for it. Are you prepared to do that?'

Jake could still feel that churning sense of elation at the prospect of escape, all mixed up with what had felt like a shameful nervousness about leaving everything familiar behind. There had been anger and resentment, too, mostly with Rupert, but also with Cassie, whose clumsy attempt to make Rupert jealous had precipitated the fight, and the offer that would change his life if he was brave enough to take it.

'The upshot was that Sir Ian said that he would sponsor me through university if I wanted the chance to start afresh somewhere new,' he told Cassie. 'It was an extraordinarily generous offer,' he said. 'It was my chance to escape from Portrevick, and I took it. I walked out of the Hall and didn't look back.'

'Was that when...?' Cassie stopped, realising too late where the question was leading, and a smile touched Jake's mouth.

'When you accosted me on my bike?' he suggested.

Cassie could feel herself turning pink, but she could hardly pretend now that she didn't remember that kiss. 'I seem to remember it was *you* who accosted *me*, wasn't it?' she said with as much dignity as she could, and Jake's smile deepened.

'I was provoked,' he excused himself.

'*Provoked?*' Cassie sat up straight, embarrassment forgotten in outrage. 'I did *not* provoke you!'

'You certainly did,' said Jake coolly. 'I wasn't in the mood to listen to you defending Rupert. He asked for that punch, and it was only because he was all set to report me to the police that Sir Ian suggested I leave Portrevick.

'That turned out to be the best thing that could have happened to me,' he allowed. 'And I'm grateful in retrospect. But it didn't feel like that at the time. It felt as if Rupert could behave as badly as he liked and that silver spoon would stay firmly stuck in his mouth. I knew nobody would ever suggest that *Rupert* should leave everything he'd ever known and work for his living. I was angry, excited and confused, and I'm afraid you got in the way.'

He paused and looked straight at Cassie, the dark-blue eyes gleaming with unmistakable amusement. 'If it's any comfort, that kiss was my last memory of Portrevick.'

That kiss… The memory of it shimmered between them, so vividly that for one jangling moment it was as if they were kissing again, as if his fingers were still twined in her hair, her lips still parting as she melted into him, that wicked excitement still tumbling along her veins.

With an effort, Cassie dragged her gaze away and buried her burning face in her coffee cup. 'Nice to know that I was memorable,' she muttered.

'You were certainly that,' said Jake.

'Yes, well, it was all a long time ago.' Cassie cleared her throat and cast around for something, anything, to change the subject. 'I'd no idea Sir Ian helped you like that,' she managed at last, seizing on the first thing she could think of. 'We all assumed you'd just taken off to avoid the assault charges.'

'That doesn't surprise me. Portrevick was always ready to think the worst of me,' said Jake, gathering up the debris of their lunch. 'Sir Ian wasn't the type to boast about his generosity, but I kept in touch all the time, and as soon as I was in a position to do so I offered to repay all the money he'd spent on my education. He flatly refused to take it, but he did say there was one thing I could do for him, and that was when he asked me to be his executor and the trustee. He asked me if I would make sure that the Portrevick estate stayed intact. You know how much he loved the Hall.'

Cassie nodded. 'Yes, he did.'

'I can't say I liked the idea of taking on a complicated trust, and I knew how much Rupert would resent me, but I owed Sir Ian too much to refuse. So,' said Jake, 'that's why we're driving down this motorway. That's why I want to get the Hall established as a venue. Once it's up and running, and self-supporting, I'll feel as if I've paid my debt to him at last. I'll have done what Sir Ian asked me to do, and then I really can put Portrevick and the past behind me once and for all.'

He drained his coffee and shoved the sandwich wrappers inside the empty cup. 'Have you finished? We've still got a long way to go, so let's hit the road again.'

Cassie studied Portrevick Hall with affection as she cut across the grounds to the sweep of gravel at its imposing entrance. A rambling manor-house dating back to the middle ages, it had grown organically as succeeding generations had added a wing here, a turret there. The result was a muddle of architectural styles that time had blended into a harmonious if faintly dilapidated whole, with crumbling terraces looking out over what had once been landscaped gardens.

It was charming from any angle, Cassie decided, and would make a wonderful backdrop for wedding photos.

Her feet crunched on the gravel as she walked up to the front door and pulled the ancient bell, deliberately avoiding looking at where Jake had sat astride his motorbike that day. She wouldn't have been at all surprised to see the outline of her feet still scorched into the stones.

Don't think about it, she told herself sternly. She was supposed to be impressing Jake with her professionalism, and she was going to have to try a lot harder today after babbling on in the car yesterday. Jake had dropped her at Tina's and driven off with barely a goodbye, and Cassie didn't blame him. He must have been sick of listening to her inane chatter for seven hours.

So today she was going to concentrate on being cool, calm and competent.

Which was easily said but harder to remember, when Jake opened the door and her heart gave a sickening lurch . He was wearing jeans and a blue Guernsey with the sleeves pushed above his wrists; without the business suit he looked younger and more approachable.

And very attractive.

'Come in,' he said. 'I was just making coffee. Do you want some?'

'Thanks.' Cassie followed him down a long, stone-flagged corridor to the Hall's vast kitchen. Without those unsettling blue eyes on her face, she could admire his lean figure and easy stride.

'Quite a looker now, isn't he?' Tina had said when they were catching up over a bottle of wine the night before. 'And rich too, I hear. You should go for it, Cassie. You always did have a bit of a thing for him.'

'No, I didn't!' said Cassie, ruffled. A thing for Jake Trevelyan? The very idea!

'Remember that Allantide Ball…?' Tina winked. 'I'm sure Jake does. Do you think you could be in with a chance?'

'No,' said Cassie, and then was horrified to hear how glum she sounded about it. 'I mean, no,' she tried again brightly. 'He's already got a perfect girlfriend.'

'Shame,' said Tina.

And the worst thing was that a tiny bit of Cassie was thinking the same thing as she watched Jake making the coffee.

Which was very unprofessional of her.

Giving herself a mental slap, Cassie pulled out her Netbook and made a show of looking around the kitchen. They might as well get down to business straight away.

'The kitchen will need replacing as a priority,' she said.

'You couldn't do professional catering in here. There's plenty of space, which is good, but it needs gutting and proper catering equipment installed.'

Jake could see that made sense. 'Get some quotes.' He nodded.

Cassie tapped in 'kitchen—get quotes' and felt efficient.

'We should start with the great hall and see how much work needs to be done there,' she went on, encouraged. 'That's the obvious place for wedding ceremonies.'

'Fine by me,' said Jake, handing her a mug. 'Let's take our coffee with us.'

The great hall had been the heart of the medieval house, but its stone walls had been panelled in the seventeenth century, and a grand wooden-staircase now swept down from a gallery on the first floor. At one end, a vast fireplace dominated an entire wall, and there was a dais at the other.

'Perfect for the high table,' said Cassie, pointing at it with her mug. Netbook under one arm, coffee clutched in her other hand, she turned slowly, imagining the space filled with people. 'They'll love this,' she enthused. 'I can see it being really popular for winter weddings.

'I always dreamed about having a Christmas wedding here,' she confided to Jake, who was also looking around, but with a lot less enthusiasm. 'There was going to be a fire burning, an enormous Christmas tree with lights, candles everywhere... Outside it would be cold and dark, but in here it would be warm and cosy.'

Funny how she could remember that fantasy so vividly after all this time. In her dream, Cassie was up there on the dais, looking beautiful and elegant—naturally—with Rupert, who gazed tenderly down at her. Her family were gathered round, bursting with pride in her, and Sir Ian was there, too, beaming with delight.

Cassie sighed.

'Anyway, I think it could look wonderful, don't you?'

Jake's mouth turned down as he studied the hall. 'Not really. It looks pretty dingy and gloomy to me.'

'That's because it's been empty for a while, and it needs a good clean. You've got to use your imagination,' said Cassie. Perching on an immense wooden trestle-table, she laid the Netbook down and sipped at her own coffee. It was cool in the hall, and she was glad of the warmth.

'It wouldn't be so different from the Allantide Ball,' she said. 'Remember how Sir Ian used to decorate it with candles and apples and it looked really inviting?'

Then she wished that she hadn't mentioned the Allantide Ball. In spite of herself, her eyes flickered to where Jake had been standing that night. She had been over by the stairs when she had spotted him. She could retrace her route across the floor, aware of the dark-blue eyes watching her approach, and a sharp little frisson shivered down her spine just as it had ten years ago.

And over there was the door leading out to the terrace… Cassie remembered the mixture of panic and excitement as Jake had taken her hand and led her out into the dark. She could still feel his hard hands on her, still feel her heart jerking frantically, and her blood still pounded at the devastating sureness of his lips.

Swallowing, she risked a glance at Jake and found her gaze snared on his. He was watching her with a faint, mocking smile, and although nothing was said she knew—she just *knew*—that he was remembering that kiss, too. The very air seemed to be jangling with the memory of that wretched ball, and Cassie wrenched her eyes away. What on earth had possessed her to mention it?

She sipped her coffee, trying desperately to think of something to say to break the awkward silence, and show Jake that she hadn't forgotten that she was here to do a job.

'What would you think about holding an Allantide Ball this year?' she said, starting slowly but gathering pace as she realised that the idea, born of desperation, might not be such a bad one after all. 'As a kind of memorial to Sir Ian? It would be good publicity.'

'No one would come,' said Jake. 'I'm not exactly popular in Portrevick. I went into the pub the last time I came down and there was dead silence when I walked in. I felt about as welcome as a cup of cold sick.'

Cassie had gathered something of that from Tina. Apparently there was much speculation in the village about Sir Ian's will, and the general feeling was that Jake had somehow pulled a fast one for his own nefarious purposes, in keeping with the Trevelyan tradition.

'That's because they don't know the truth,' she said. 'Inviting everyone to the ball for Sir Ian and explaining what you're planning for the Hall would make them see that you're not just out to make a quick buck. You need the locals on your side if the wedding venue is to be a success,' she went on persuasively. 'I think this would be a great way to kick things off.'

CHAPTER FOUR

'I'M DAMNED if I'm going to waste my time sucking up to Portrevick,' said Jake, a mulish look about his mouth..

'You won't have to. I'll do it for you,' said Cassie soothingly. 'You won't need to do anything but turn up on 31st October, put on a tux and be civil for two or three hours. You can manage that, can't you?'

'I suppose so,' he said grudgingly.

'It'll be worth it when you can walk away and know the Hall is established as part of the community and has local support,' she encouraged him. 'If you want to fulfil Sir Ian's wishes, then this is the best way you can go about it.'

Jake looked at her; she was sitting on the old table and swinging her legs. She was a vibrant figure in the gloomy hall with her bright cardigan, bright face and bright, unruly hair. She didn't look sensible, but he had a feeling that what she had said just might be.

'It's not long to Allantide,' he pointed out. 'You'll never get contractors in that quickly.'

'We will if you're prepared to pay for it,' said Cassie, gaining confidence with every word. 'We've got six weeks. If we aimed to have the great hall redecorated by then, it would give us a real incentive to get things moving.'

Narrowing her eyes, she pictured the hall decorated and full of people. 'It's not as if any major structural work is required. It just needs cleaning up a bit.'

She flicked open her Netbook and began typing notes to herself. This was good. There had been a nasty little wobble there when she'd remembered the time they had kissed, but she was feeling under control again now. Cool, calm, competent; wasn't that how she was supposed to be?

OK, maybe she wasn't *calm*, exactly—not with the unsettling feeling that seemed to fizz under her skin whenever she looked at Jake—but at least she was giving a good impression of competence for once.

'The more I think about it, the more I like the idea,' she said. 'We can use the ball to start spreading the word that the Hall can be hired for special occasions. We'll invite the local paper here to take some pictures…oh! And we can have some photos done for a website too, so people can see how fabulous the great hall can look. We can hardly put a picture up of it looking the way it does now, can we?'

'Website?' said Jake, a little taken aback at how quickly her plans seemed to be developing.

'You've got to have a website,' Cassie said as if stating the obvious. 'In fact, we should think about that right away. We can't afford to leave it until all the work's been done, or we'll miss out on another year.'

Fired with enthusiasm, she snapped the Netbook closed and jumped off the table. 'Come on, let's look at the other rooms.'

She dragged Jake round the entire house, looking into every room and getting more and more excited as she went.

'You know, I really think this could be fantastic,' she said when they ended up on the terraces outside. She gestured expansively. 'You've got everything: a wonderfully old and romantic place for ceremonies, enough space for big parties, plenty of bedrooms…

'We don't need to do them all at once,' she reassured Jake, who had been mentally calculating how much all these grand plans were going to cost. 'At first, we just need somewhere the bride can get ready, but eventually we could offer rooms for the whole wedding-party.'

'Maybe,' said Jake, unwilling to commit himself too far at this stage. He wanted the Hall to become self-sufficient so he didn't need to think about it any more, but it was becoming evident as Cassie outlined her ideas that it was going to prove a lot more expensive than he had first anticipated.

'And the best thing is, there's no major structural work required yet,' she went on. 'We just need to think about the initial refurbishment for now.'

She pointed over towards the fine nineteenth-century stable block with older barns beyond. 'Eventually you could have more than one wedding at a time. The barns would be great for an informal wedding.'

Her face was alight with enthusiasm, and Jake found himself thinking that perhaps giving Cassie the contract might not be such a big mistake after all.

Last night, he had bitterly regretted that he had ever taken the advice to contact her. Cassie had talked all the way down the motorway, barely drawing breath for seven whole hours. She had an extraordinarily vivid imagination and was, Jake had to admit, very funny at times. But she was much too distracting. He had been exasperated by the way she kept tugging at the edge of his vision when he should have been concentrating on the road.

Now he was changing his mind again. Perhaps Cassie wasn't as coolly professional as the people he normally did business with, but she seemed to know what she was talking about. Her speech was refreshingly free of business jargon, and she had a warmth and an enthusiasm that might in the end get the job done faster than one of his marketing team, however sound their grasp of financial imperatives or strategic analysis.

She was leaning on the terrace wall, looking out over garden, her hands resting on the crumbling coping-stones. In profile, her lashes were long and tilting, the edge of her mouth a dreamy curve. The sunlight glinted on her brown curls—except that brown was too dull a word for her hair, Jake realised. Funny how he had never noticed what a beautiful colour it was before, a shade somewhere between auburn and chestnut with hints of honey and gold.

Unaware of his gaze, Cassie was following her own train of thought. 'I've just had a great idea!' she said, turning to him, and Jake looked quickly away. 'I've got contacts with a couple of wedding magazines. Maybe I could get them to do a story about how we're turning the Hall into the ultimate wedding venue? It would be fantastic promotion and get people talking about it. We could even start taking some advance bookings... What do you think?'

'I think I'm going to leave it all up to you,' said Jake slowly.

'Really?' The big brown eyes lit with excitement.

'Yes,' he said, making up his mind. He doubted that he would find anyone else as committed to the project, even if he had the time to find them. 'We can agree the fees when we get back to London, but in the meantime I'd like you to go ahead, make whatever decisions you need and get work started as soon as possible.'

'Er...it's me.' Cassie made a face at the phone. *Excellent, Cassie.* Stuttering and stumbling was always a good way to impress an important client with your professionalism. 'Cassie... Cassandra Grey,' she added, just in case Jake knew anyone else who went to pieces at the sound of his voice.

'Yes, so my PA said when she put you through,' said Jake with an edge of impatience.

'Oh yes, I suppose she did. Um, well, I just thought I'd let you know how things are going at the Hall.'

'Yes?'

His voice was clipped, and Cassie bit her lip, furious with herself for irritating him before she had even started. Why was she being so moronic? Everything was working out just as she'd planned, and she had been feeling really pleased with herself. Ringing Jake with an update hadn't seemed like a big deal when she had picked up the phone two minutes ago, but the minute he had barked his name her insides had jerked themselves into a knot of nerves.

He sounded so distant that she was tempted to put the phone down, but that would be even sillier. Besides, she needed his OK on a number of matters.

'We've been making progress,' she told him brightly.

'Yes?' he said again, and her heart sank. She had hoped they had reached a kind of understanding at the Hall. Jake had certainly seemed more approachable then, but he was obviously in a vile mood now—which didn't bode well for the idea she wanted to put to him.

She cleared her throat. 'There are one or two things I need to talk to you about,' she said. 'Are you free for lunch at all this week?'

'Is it important?'

What did he think—that she wanted to take him out for the pleasure of his company? Wisely, Cassie held her tongue.

'It is, rather.'

There was an exasperated sigh at the other end of the phone, and she imagined him checking his electronic organiser. 'Does it have to be this week?'

Clearly, he couldn't wait to see her again. 'The sooner the better, really,' said Cassie.

More tsking. 'Lunch might be tricky,' he said after a moment. 'Could we make it dinner instead?'

Oh, great. And there she had been feeling nervous at the prospect of an hour's lunch. 'Er, yes. Of course.'

'What about tomorrow?'

'Fine. I'll book a table,' said Cassie quickly, just so he knew that it was a business dinner and that she would be picking up the tab. Not that there was any question of a date.

She hesitated. 'As it's dinner, would Natasha like to join us?' she asked delicately.

There was a pause. 'Not tomorrow,' said Jake curtly.

'Oh, that's a pity,' said Cassie, although actually she was rather glad. She didn't fancy spending a whole evening being compared to the perfect Natasha, and besides she couldn't help feeling that her idea would be better put to Jake alone in the first instance.

They arranged to meet at Giovanni's, an Italian restaurant just round the corner from Avalon's office, where she and Joss were regulars. There was no way Cassie's expense account could rise to the kind of restaurants Jake was no doubt accustomed to, but the food at Giovanni's was good and the ambience cheerful, and in the end Cassie decided that it was better to stick to the unpretentious.

It was only when she arrived the following evening that she began to wonder if it had been such a good idea. Giovanni treated her and Joss like daughters, and the brides-to-be they took there were invariably delighted by him, but Cassie had a feeling Jake would be less charmed.

Still, it was too late to change now. Cassie hurried along the street, her heels clicking on the pavement. Anxious not to make it look as if she were expecting some kind of date, but wanting to make an effort for their now most-important client, she had dithered too long about what to wear. Eventually she had decided on a sleeveless dress with a little cardigan and her favourite suede boots, but they had proved to be a mistake, too. Fabulous as they were, it was hard to walk very fast in them.

Jake, of course, hadn't even had the decency to be a few minutes late and was waiting for her outside Giovanni's, looking dark, lean and remote. His suit was immaculately tailored, his expression shuttered. Oh God, now he was cross with her for not being on time.

Cassie's heart sank further. It didn't look as if the evening was getting off to a good start.

'I'm *so* sorry,' she said breathlessly as she clicked up on her heels. 'I hope you haven't been waiting long?'

'A couple of minutes, that's all. I was early.'

The dark gaze rested on her face and Cassie saw herself in his eyes, red-faced and puffing, her hair all anyhow. So much for cool professionalism. She had been so proud of herself recently, too, and had vowed that it would be the start of a whole new image.

'Well, let's go in.' Flustered, she reached for the door, intending to stand back and usher Jake through, but Jake was too quick for her. He reached an arm behind her and held the door, leaving Cassie no option but to go ahead of him. It was that or an unseemly tussle, but as it was she was left looking like the little woman rather than the cool, capable businesswoman she wanted to be.

No, *not* a good start.

Giovanni spied her across the restaurant and came sailing over to greet her, his arms outstretched.

'Cassie! *Bella!*' His kissed her soundly on both cheeks before holding her away from him. 'You're looking too thin,' he scolded her, the way he always did, before turning his beady gaze on Jake. 'And who is this?' he asked interestedly. 'It's about time you brought a man here!'

'Mr Trevelyan is a *client*, Giovanni,' said Cassie hastily.

'Shame!' he whispered to her, plucking a couple of menus from the bar. 'He looks your type, I think.'

Cassie opened her mouth to protest that Jake was most certainly *not* her type, but realised just in time that she could hardly embark on an argument with Jake right there. She would just have to hope that he hadn't heard. He hadn't recoiled in horror, anyway. In fact, he didn't seem to be paying them much attention at all, which was a little irritating in one way, but a big relief in another.

So she contented herself with crossing her eyes and giving Giovanni a warning glare, which he ignored completely as he gestured them towards a table tucked away in a little alcove where a candle flickered invitingly. It looked warm and intimate, and perfect for lovers.

'My best table for you,' he said, handing them the menus with a flourish. 'Nice and quiet so you can talk to your *client*,' he added to Cassie with an outrageous wink.

At least the dim lighting hid her scarlet cheeks. Cassie was mortified. 'Did I mention Joss and I were thinking of taking our clients to the Thai restaurant next door in future?' she muttered, but Giovanni only laughed.

'I will bring you some wine and Roberto will take your order and then, don't worry, you can be quite alone...' Chuckling to himself, he surged off to the kitchen, leaving a little pool of silence behind him.

Cassie unfolded her napkin. 'I'm sorry about that,' she said awkwardly after a moment. 'He's quite a character.'

'So I gather,' said Jake.

'I mean, he's lovely, but he does go a bit far sometimes. We bring a lot of clients here, but it's usually at lunchtime, and they're usually brides, so it's become a bit of a standing joke that I never come with a boyfriend.'

She trailed off, horribly aware that she was babbling. Jake was making her nervous. There was a tightness to him tonight, a grim set to his mouth, and an air of suppressed anger. Surely it wasn't anything she had done, was it? Everything had been going so well down in Portrevick. Had he heard something?

'Er, well, anyway... We're supposed to be talking about the Hall,' she said brightly.

Jake seemed to focus on her properly for the first time. 'You said you had made some progress?'

'I have.' Cassie told him about the contractors she had engaged. A small army of them was already hard at work. 'They're mostly cleaners,' she explained. 'There's so much wood in the great hall that it doesn't need much decorating—

although they're repainting the roof—but the walls, the floor and the fireplace need a thorough clean and polish. It's all well in hand for the Allantide Ball.'

'Good,' said Jake absently. Cassie wondered if he had even been listening. He was frowning down at a knife he was spinning beneath one finger.

'I've also been in touch with various local caterers, florists, photographers and so on, and started to draw up a directory of our own.'

'It all sounds very promising,' said Jake as Giovanni's nephew appeared with a carafe of wine. Less expansive than his uncle, or perhaps just more sensitive to Jake's grim expression, he took their orders with the minimum of fuss.

'You've been busy,' Jake added to Cassie, folding the menu and handing it back to the waiter.

Well, at least he had been listening. She had wondered there for a minute. 'There's lots to do, but I'm enjoying it.'

Jake reached for the carafe, but, mindful that she was supposed to be the host, Cassie got there first, and he watched without comment as she filled two glasses. She didn't know about Jake, but she certainly needed one!

She drew a breath. 'I've been thinking about a promotion, too.'

If only Jake was in a more amenable mood, she thought. It was going to be tricky enough breaking the news of the deal she had made with *Wedding Belles* as it was. She took a sip of wine to fortify herself. 'Do you remember me saying it might be worth contacting a couple of magazines in case they wanted to run a piece about setting up the Hall as a venue?' she began cautiously.

'Vaguely.'

It was hardly the most encouraging of responses, but Cassie ploughed on anyway. 'Well, I did that, and one of them is very keen on the idea.'

There was a pause. Jake could see that she was waiting

for him to say something, although he wasn't sure what. 'OK,' he said.

'But they want a bit more of a human-interest angle.'

'Human interest?'

'Yes, you know, to personalise the story? So it's not just the story of how the building is being prepared, it's also about a couple preparing to get married there. The readers love real-life stories,' Cassie hurried on. 'The editor of *Wedding Belles*—that's the magazine—wants to follow a couple who are going to be married there. So the article will be illustrated with pictures of them choosing the flowers, planning menus, trying on wedding dresses and all that kind of thing.'

'But we haven't got any couples yet,' Jake objected. 'Surely the whole point of promoting the Hall like this is to *find* someone who wants to get married there?'

'Quite,' said Cassie, relieved that he at least could see the point of the article. 'We haven't got any punters yet, but we *have* got you and Natasha…' She trailed off, hoping that Jake would get where this was all going.

He had gone very still. 'What about me and Natasha?'

'OK, I *may* have stretched the truth a little bit here,' Cassie acknowledged, and took the final hurdle in a rush. 'But the editor was so keen on the idea that I told her that you were getting married at the Hall at Christmas.'

'*What?*'

Jake's voice was like a lash, and carried right across the restaurant. Diners on nearby tables turned to look at them in surprise, and behind Jake at the bar Giovanni clutched a hand to his heart with an exaggerated expression of sympathy for her.

Cassie glowered at him and turned deliberately back to Jake. She had been afraid he might react like that.

'I know it's a cheek,' she said, holding up her hands in a placatory gesture. 'But I really do think it would be great publicity for the Hall. And you don't have to go through with it if Natasha doesn't want to get married there. They'll only want pictures of a few set occasions, so I don't see any reason why we shouldn't set up a few shots and create a story for them.'

Jake was looking grimly discouraging, so she hurried on before he could give her a flat no. 'We don't need to tell them that it isn't actually the dress Natasha is going to wear, or those aren't really the flowers she'd choose,' she reassured him. 'You and Natasha would just be models, if you like, showing what a wonderful wedding-venue the Hall will be. I know you're both busy, but it shouldn't take up too much time. Just a few hours every now and then to have your photos taken.

'It would be a really effective way to promote the Hall,' Cassie went on when there was still no response from Jake. There was an edge of desperation in her voice by now. It had taken ages to get the editor of *Wedding Belles* to agree to feature Portrevick Hall, and it was only the promise of the human interest lent by the owner himself getting married there—another little stretching of the truth—that had swung it for her.

'You did say you wanted the venue to be self-sustaining as soon as possible,' she reminded him. '*Wedding Belles* is really popular with brides-to-be around the country, and its circulation figures are amazing. If they run a feature about the Hall, we'll have couples queuing up to book it, and you'll be able to hand the whole place over to a manager much sooner than you thought.'

Jake drank some wine, then put down his glass. 'There's just one problem,' he said.

'Just one?' said Cassie, trying to lighten the atmosphere. 'That doesn't sound too bad!'

He didn't smile back. 'Unfortunately it's quite a major one,' he said. 'I'm afraid Natasha isn't around to model anything any more. She's left me.'

Cassie put down her glass so abruptly, wine sloshed onto the tablecloth. 'Natasha's *left* you?'

'So it seems.'

'But…but…' Cassie was floundering. It was the last thing she had expected to hear. 'God, I'm so sorry! I had no idea…' No wonder Jake was looking so grim! 'When did all this happen?'

'When I got back from Cornwall.' Jake reached across with his napkin and mopped up the wine Cassie had spilt before she made even more of a mess. 'Natasha was waiting for me with her case packed. She said she was sorry, but she had met someone else and fallen madly in love with him.'

His first reaction had been one of surprise at her words. Natasha had never been the type to do anything *madly*. One of the things he had always liked about her was her calm, rational approach to everything, and now it seemed as if she was just as illogical and emotional as, well, as Cassie.

'How awful for you.' Cassie's round face was puckered with sympathy. 'How long had it been going on?'

'Hardly any time. She said he'd literally swept her off her feet. I'll bet he did,' Jake added grimly. 'He's had plenty of practice.'

'Gosh, he's not a friend of yours, is he?' That would make it twice as humiliating for him.

'A friend?' Jake gave a short, mirthless laugh. 'Hardly! Rupert Branscombe Fox is no friend of mine.'

'*Rupert?*' Cassie's eyes were out on stalks. Crikey, this was like something out of a soap opera! 'But how on earth did Natasha meet Rupert?'

'It was my own fault,' said Jake. Funnily enough, now that he'd started talking, he didn't feel too bad. He'd been so angry before that he could barely bite out a word. 'I invited Rupert round to discuss the trust at home, and Natasha was there. I didn't think she was that impressed with him at the time.'

Cassie remembered now. Perfect Natasha had decided that Rupert was shallow—or that was what she had said, anyway.

'What changed her mind?'

'Rupert did. He deliberately set out to seduce Natasha to get at me.' Jake's expression was set. 'I can't believe she fell for it,' he said, sounding genuinely baffled. 'I thought she was too sensible to have her head turned by Rupert's very super-ficial attraction. I can't understand it at all.'

Cassie could. Even as a boy, Rupert had been extraordinarily good-looking, and if he had turned the full battery of his sex appeal on Natasha he must have been well nigh irresistible. Perhaps Natasha had been tired of being told how admirably sensible she was.

But poor Jake. How hurt and angry he must have been!

'Rupert's very…charming,' she said lamely.

Jake tossed back his wine and poured himself another glass. 'He's *using* Natasha. I can't believe she can't see it for herself!'

'Maybe he's fallen in love with her,' Cassie suggested

'Love?' Jake snorted. 'Rupert doesn't love anyone but himself.'

'You don't *know* that—'

'Sure I do,' he interrupted her. 'Rupert was kind enough to explain it to me. Natasha was perfect for his purposes, he said. He was furious and humiliated by the trust Sir Ian had set up, and he's chosen to blame me for it. Breaking up my relationship with Natasha was doubly sweet. It hurt me, and it gives him access to the trust money, or so he thinks. He claims he's going to marry her because I won't have any grounds for arguing that Natasha isn't a sensible woman, as specified by Sir Ian. He was quite sure I would understand, *old chap*.'

Ouch. Cassie grimaced at the savagery in Jake's voice. She didn't blame him for being angry. She could practically hear Rupert's light, cut-glass tones, and could just imagine what effect they would have had on Jake.

'What are you going to do?'

'Well, I'm certainly not handing over the money yet. Natasha deserves better than to be married for such a cynical reason. The moment Rupert's got his hands on the money, he'll dump her like the proverbial ton of bricks,' said Jake. 'He's still got to prove to me that he's settled down, and I'll believe that when I see it!'

Under the circumstances, it was generous of him to still think about Natasha, Cassie thought. He must love her, even if she had proved to be not quite as perfect as he had believed.

Cassie pushed her glass around, making patterns on the tablecloth. It would be quite something to be loved by someone like Jake, who didn't give up on you even when you made a terrible mistake. She wondered if Natasha would realise that once the first thrill of being with Rupert wore off.

As it inevitably would. Cassie wasn't a fool, whatever her family thought. She had long ago realised that Rupert's appeal lay largely in the fact that he was out of reach. He was so impossibly handsome, so extraordinarily charming, so unbelievably glamorous, that you couldn't imagine doing anything ordinary with him. He was the kind of man you dreamed of having a mad, passionate affair with, not the kind of man you lived with and loved every day.

Not like Jake.

Cassie's fingers stilled on the glass. Where had *that* thought come from?

Looking up from her wine, she studied him across the table. Lost in his own thoughts, he was broodingly turning a fork on the tablecloth, his own head bent and the dark, stormy eyes hidden. She could see the angular planes of his face, the jut of his nose, the set of his mouth, and all at once it was as if she had never seen him before.

There was a solidity and a control to him, she realised, disconcerted to realise that she could imagine living with him in a way she had never been able to with Rupert. Bumping into Rupert again had been one of her favourite fantasies for years, but in her dreams they were never doing anything ordinary. They were *getting* married, not *being* married. They were going to Paris or sitting on a yacht in the Caribbean, not having breakfast or watching television or emptying the dishwasher.

How strange that she could picture Jake in her flat, could

see him coming in from work, taking off his jacket, loosening his tie, reaching for her with a smile…

A strange shiver snaked its way down her spine. It was just Jake, she reminded herself. But he was so immediate, so real, so *there*, that his presence felt like a hand against her skin, and all at once she was struggling to drag enough oxygen into her lungs.

And then he looked up, the dark-blue eyes locked with hers, and she forgot to breathe at all.

'Spaghetti carbonara.'

Cassie actually jumped as Giovanni deposited a steaming plate in front of her.

'And fettucine *all'arrabiata* for your *client*!'

She barely noticed Giovanni's jovial winks and nods of encouragement as he fussed around with pepper and parmesan. How long had she been staring into Jake's eyes, unable to look away? A second? Ten? Ten *minutes*? She hoped it was the first, but it was impossible to tell. She felt oddly jarred, and her heart was knocking erratically against her ribs.

She was terrified in case Jake was able to read her thoughts in her eyes. Of course, she would have known if he had, because he would look absolutely horrified. He probably couldn't think of anything worse than going home to her in an untidy flat every night.

Why was *that* a depressing thought?

CHAPTER FIVE

AND why was she even *thinking* about it? Cassie asked herself crossly as she picked up her fork. Disappointed by her lack of response, Giovanni had taken himself off at last. Jake was obviously still in love with the not-quite-so-perfect Natasha, who had had her sensible head turned by Rupert.

Twirling spaghetti in her spoon, she forced her mind back to the conversation. 'I'm really sorry,' she said when Giovanni had left. 'If it's any comfort, I don't imagine Rupert will be easy to live with. Perhaps Natasha will change her mind.'

'That's what I'm hoping,' said Jake.

That wasn't quite what Cassie had been hoping to hear. *I wouldn't take her back if she grovelled from here to Friday* was more what she had had in mind.

She sighed inwardly. Stop being so silly, she told herself.

'In the meantime, I'll go back to *Wedding Belles* and tell them that we'd still like a feature on the Hall, but we can't manage the human-interest angle.'

Jake's gaze sharpened. 'I thought you said they wouldn't do a piece without that?'

'No, well, it's not the end of the world. We can find other ways of promoting the Hall.'

'They won't reach the same market, though?'

'Probably not.'

Jake brooded, stirring his fork mindlessly around in the fettucine. 'To hell with it!' he said explosively after a while and looked up at Cassie, who regarded him warily. 'I'm damned if I'm going to let Rupert mess up my plans for the Hall, too. He's made enough trouble! I say we go ahead with it anyway.'

'We can't do much about it without Natasha,' she reminded him reluctantly.

'Unless…' Jake trailed off, staring at Cassie as if seeing her properly for the first time.

She stared back, more than a little unnerved. 'What?'

'Did you tell this editor Natasha's name?'

'No, I didn't go into details. I just said the owner of the Hall was getting married.'

'So I don't really need Natasha—I just need a fiancée?'

'Well, yes, but—'

'So why don't I marry you?'

There was a rushing sound in Cassie's ears. She went hot, then cold, then hot again. 'Me?' she squeaked. 'You don't want to marry me!'

'Of course I don't,' said Jake, recoiling. 'God, no! But you said yourself that it doesn't have to be a real engagement. If all we need is to have a few photographs taken, why shouldn't you be the bride-to-be?'

'Well, because—because—' Cassie stuttered, groping for all the glaringly obvious reasons why she couldn't, and bizarrely unable to think of any. 'Because everyone would know it wasn't true.'

'You just said you didn't give the magazine any names.'

'I wasn't thinking of them. I was thinking of all the people who know perfectly well we're not engaged.'

'Who's going to know?'

'Anyone who sees the article,' she said, exasperated, but Jake only looked down his nose.

'I don't know anyone who's likely to read *Wedding Belles*,' he said.

Cassie glared at him. 'It's not just about you, though, is it? I know masses of people who read it for one reason or another, and if one of my friends gets whiff of the fact that I'm apparently engaged without telling anyone I'll never hear the end of it!'

Jake couldn't see the problem. 'The article won't be published until next year,' he said dismissively. 'We can worry about what we tell people then. Rupert will never stick with Natasha for more than a few weeks, so there'll be no reason not to tell everyone the truth then. We'll say it was just a marketing exercise.'

'And what about when the *Wedding Belles* photographer comes down to take pictures of us supposedly planning our wedding at the Hall?' asked Cassie, picking up her spoon and fork once more. 'It'll be all over Portrevick in no time. You know what the village is like. We'd never be able to keep it secret. Rupert's got some fancy weekend place in St Ives; what's the betting he'll hear about it?'

'What if he does? It wouldn't do him any harm to think that I'm not inconsolable.'

'No, but if he gets wind of the fact that you're just pretending…' Cassie trailed off and Jake nodded.

'You're right,' he said. 'Rupert wouldn't hesitate to make trouble for me in whatever way he could.' He looked across the table at Cassie. 'In that case, let's make it true,' he said.

She stared at him. 'What do you mean?'

'Let's make it a real engagement,' he said, as if it were the most obvious thing in the world. 'Or, at least, not a secret one,' he amended. 'We can tell everybody who needs to know, and do the photographs for the article quite openly. We'll know it's not a real engagement, but we don't have to tell anyone else that.'

Let's make it a real engagement. Cassie was furious with

herself for the way her heart had jumped at his words, in spite of the fact that only a matter of minutes ago he had been recoiling in horror at the very idea. 'Nobody would believe it,' she said flatly.

'Why not?'

'Come on, Jake. I'm hardly your type, am I? Are you really going to ask people to believe you took one look at me and fell in love with me? They'd know it wasn't true.'

'Oh, I don't know.' Jake studied her over the rim of his glass. It was warm in the restaurant, and she had shrugged off the silky cardigan, leaving her shoulders bare. She was a warm, glowing figure in the candlelight. 'I can think of more unlikely scenarios,' he said.

His gaze flustered Cassie, and she tore her eyes away to concentrate fiercely on twisting spaghetti around her fork. 'Sure,' she said. 'And when was this supposed to have happened?'

'How about when you walked into my office and fell into my arms?'

Cassie felt her colour rising at the memory. 'And you thought, "I've been waiting all my life for someone clumsy to come along"?'

'Perhaps I've had a thing about you since I kissed you at the Allantide Ball,' Jake suggested. 'Perhaps I've been waiting ten years to find you again.'

It was clear that he was being flippant, but there was an undercurrent of *something* in his voice. Cassie did everything she could to stop herself looking up to meet his eyes again, but it was hopeless. Something stronger than her was dragging her gaze up from the fork to lock with Jake's. She could almost hear the click as it snapped into place.

His eyes were dark and unreadable in the candlelight, but still her heart began that silly pattering again, while her pulse throbbed alarmingly.

She swallowed. 'I don't think that sounds very likely either.'

'Well, then, we'll tell it exactly as it was,' said Jake, sounding infuriatingly normal. How come *his* heart wasn't lurching all over the place at the very thought of falling in love with her? He clearly wasn't having any trouble breathing, either.

'We met when you came to discuss developing the Hall as a wedding venue. Then we drove down to Portrevick together.'

'And on the way we fell madly in love and agreed to get married right away?' said Cassie, who had managed to look away again at last.

Jake shrugged away her scorn. 'You're the one who believes in that kind of thing,' he reminded her. 'If we say that's what happened, why would anyone believe it wasn't true?'

'I can't believe you're making it all sound so reasonable,' she protested.

How had they got to this point? It was as if the whole evening had been turned on its head. When she arrived, she had been cock-a-hoop at the idea of the magazine feature, and her only concern had been how to convince Jake to go for it. Now it was Jake talking her into an engagement just to make sure the article went ahead. How had that happened?

'Look, it makes sense.' Jake was clearly losing patience. 'You're the ideal person to feature in the article. You know all about weddings. You'll be able to say all the right things and make sure the Hall comes out of it looking beautiful.'

'That's true, I suppose.' Cassie looked at the fork she had laden so carefully with spaghetti and put it down. She had lost her appetite. 'But what about you?' she said hesitantly.

'What about me?'

'Won't you find it very difficult?'

'It might be a bit of a struggle to look interested in table decorations,' said Jake. 'But I expect I can manage if it's just one or two photo sessions. I won't be required to do much else, will I?'

'I wasn't thinking about that,' said Cassie. 'I was thinking about what it would be like for you to have to pretend to be happy with me when I know how you must be feeling about Natasha. I'd be devastated if it was me.'

'At least I won't look it,' said Jake, wondering how he did feel.

Angry, humiliated—yes. But *devastated*? Jake didn't think so. His overwhelming feeling, he decided, was one of disappointment in Natasha. He had been attracted by her beauty, of course, but just as much he had liked her intelligence and composure. He couldn't believe that she would lose her head over someone like Rupert, of all people.

Jake remembered telling Cassie how well he and Natasha were matched. Natasha was perfect, he had told her. And she had been. She had never irritated or distracted him the way Cassie did, for instance. She was everything he needed in a woman.

More than that, when he looked at Natasha, Jake had felt as if he had left Portrevick behind him once and for all. With a beautiful, accomplished, sexy, successful woman like Natasha on his arm, he'd been able to believe that he had made it at last.

And then Rupert Branscombe Fox had lifted his little finger and she had gone.

Jake's jaw tightened and he stared down at the wine he was swirling in his glass. Rupert's condescension could still reduce him to a state of seething resentment. Rupert in return would never forgive him for humiliating him in that stupid fight, or for being the one his uncle had entrusted with his not-inconsiderable fortune.

'Rupert wants me to be devastated,' he told Cassie. 'He wants me to feel humiliated and heartbroken. He wants me to have to tell everyone that my beautiful girlfriend has dumped me for him. I've got no intention of giving him that satisfaction.'

Jake set down his glass and looked directly at Cassie. 'You asked if I'd find it difficult to pretend to be in love with you instead of Natasha—the answer is that it wouldn't be half as hard as losing face with Rupert. I'd do anything rather than do that. I'm sorry about Natasha, but this isn't about her. It's between Rupert and me.'

'Getting engaged to me would make it look as if Rupert had done you a favour by taking Natasha off your hands,' said Cassie slowly. She knew that Jake and Rupert had never got on, but she hadn't realised the rivalry between them was still so bitter.

'Exactly,' said Jake. 'You'd be helping me to save face, and that would mean a lot to me. I'm not proud. I'll beg if you want me to.'

'I don't know.' Cassie fingered the wax dribbling down the candle uncertainly. 'If we're pretending to be engaged in Portrevick, word's bound to get back to my parents. What are they going to think if they find out I'm apparently marrying you and haven't told them?'

Jake shrugged. 'Tell them the truth, then. What does it matter if they know? They're not going to rush off to *Wedding Belles* to tell the editor their daughter is telling a big fib, are they?'

'No, but they might rush to tell Liz and my brothers that I've got myself in a stupid mess again,' said Cassie, who could imagine the conversation all too clearly: *why can Cassie never do anything properly? When is she going to grow up and get a proper job that doesn't involve silly pretences?*

'I'm sick of being the family failure,' she told Jake. 'I wanted to show them that I could be successful too. That was why I so pleased when you gave us the contract to turn the Hall into a wedding venue. I rang my parents and told them I had a real career at last.'

She squeezed a piece of wax between her fingers, remembering the warm glow of her parents' approval. 'I don't want to tell them my great new job involves pretending to be in love with you.'

'Do you want to tell them you've lost your great new job because you weren't prepared to do whatever it took to make it work?'

Cassie dropped the wax and sat back in her chair. 'Isn't that blackmail?' she said dubiously, and Jake sighed impatiently.

'It's telling you to hurry up and make a decision,' he said.

'Look, if it's such a problem, say we really *are* engaged, then when we've finished with all the photos you can tell them you've changed your mind and dumped me. If they remember me at all, I'm sure they'll be delighted to hear it,' he finished in an arid voice.

Cassie turned it over in her mind. It might work. Of course, the best scenario would be that her family never got to hear about her supposed engagement at all, but if they did get a whiff of it she could always pretend that Jake had swept her off her feet. It was only three months to Christmas. She could easily find excuses not to take him home in that time.

Tina might be a little harder to fool, especially as she was on the spot in Portrevick, but there was no reason why she shouldn't tell her old friend the truth. Tina could be trusted to keep it to herself—and besides they might need her to pretend to be the bridesmaid.

Anyway, it didn't sound as if she had a choice. Cassie wasn't entirely sure whether Jake was serious about making the engagement a condition of the contract, but she wasn't prepared to push him on it. He had been hurt by Natasha, humiliated by Rupert, and was clearly in no mood to compromise.

And really, would it be so bad? Cassie asked herself. The article had been her idea to start with, and she still believed it would be just what they needed to kick-start promotion for the Hall. Of course, she hadn't reckoned on taking such a prominent role herself, but Jake was right. She would be able to decorate the Hall exactly as she wanted without having to take Natasha's wishes into account. She could recreate her dream wedding for the article.

Cassie felt a flicker of excitement at the prospect.

It might be fun.

It wasn't as if they were planning on doing anything illegal or immoral, after all. A mock engagement would save Jake's face, ensure a lucrative contract and her job at Avalon, if not a whole new career. Why was she even hesitating?

'All right,' she said abruptly. 'I'll do it. But, if we're going to pretend to be engaged, we're going to have to do it properly,' she warned him. 'That means that when the photographer is around you'll have to be there and be prepared to look suitably besotted.'

'Don't you think I can do that?'

Jake reached across the table for her hands, taking Cassie by surprise. 'I'm sure you can,' she said, flustered, trying to tug them free, but he tightened his grip.

'I can do whatever you need me to,' he said, turning her hands over and lifting first one palm and then the other to his mouth to kiss.

Cassie felt the touch of his lips like a shock reverberating down to her toes, and she sucked in a shuddering breath.

'See?' Jake said softly, without letting go of her hands. '*I* can do it. More to the point,' he said, 'can *you*?'

The challenge hung between them, flickering in the candlelight.

Cassie swallowed hard. It was hard to think straight with his warm, strong fingers clasping hers, and the feel of his lips scorched onto her palms, but she retained enough sanity to know that the last thing she needed was to let him know how his touch affected her.

He had recoiled at the very idea of marrying her. *Of course I don't*, he had said. Cassie suspected that Jake had been more hurt by Natasha's betrayal than he was letting on. This was partly to be his revenge on her, partly a game, a pretence, a strategy to save his face and solve the problem of his unwanted responsibility for the Hall. That was all.

Which was fine. All she had to do was treat it like a game too, and remember that her strategy was to turn the Hall into the most sought-after wedding venue in the South West. She would prove to her family that she was not just a dreamer, but could be just as successful in her chosen field as they were in theirs.

So she drew her hands from Jake's and laid them instead

on either side of his face. 'Of course I can, darling,' she said, shivering at the prickle of the rough male skin beneath her fingers, and she leant forward across the table to brush a kiss against his mouth.

She felt Jake stiffen in surprise, and, although a panic-stricken part of her was screaming at her to sit back and laugh it off as a joke, another more persuasive part was noting that his lips were warm and firm and that they fitted her own perfectly, as if their mouths had been made for each other.

It felt so good to kiss him, to touch him, that Cassie pushed the panicky thoughts aside and let her lips linger on his. But that was a mistake, of course. Beneath hers, his mouth curved into a smile, and the next moment she felt his hand slide beneath her hair to hold her head still, and he began kissing her back.

And then they were kissing each other, their lips parting, their tongues twining, teasing, and Cassie murmured deep in her throat, smiling too even as she kissed him again, lost in the dizzying rush of heat and the terrifying sense of rightness.

Afterwards, she never had any idea how long that kiss had lasted. But when they broke apart at last she was thudding from the tips of her hair to her toenails, and Giovanni was standing by the table wearing a broad smile.

'Client, huh?' he said to her with a wink, but it was Jake who answered.

'Not any more,' he said. 'We just got engaged.'

Cassie tossed and turned half the night, reliving that kiss. She had gone too far, just like her mother always said she did. A brief peck on the lips would have been enough to make her point, and she could have gone back to being businesslike—but, oh no! She had had to push it. She had had to *kiss* him.

She mustn't let herself get carried away like that again, Cassie told herself sternly. This was just a pretence, and she mustn't forget it. On the other hand, her job might have depended on pretending to be engaged to a man with wet lips and clammy hands. As it was, well, she might as well enjoy the perks, mightn't she?

So she was in high good humour when she bounced into the office the next morning. She had never been engaged before. OK, she wasn't *really* engaged, and she probably ought to be feeling more cross about having been effectively blackmailed into it, but at least it meant that she didn't have any choice in the matter. If anyone—for example her super-achieving family—ever asked her how she came to do such a crazy thing, she could hold up her hands and say, 'Hey, I was forced into it.'

Or perhaps it would be better to put a more positive spin on it. She didn't want to look like a victim. She could narrow her eyes, look serious and explain that she was someone who was prepared to do anything—anything!—to get the job done.

'Well, I hope you know what you're doing,' said Joss doubtfully when Cassie tried this line on her. Joss, like Tina, had to know the truth. 'This Jake Trevelyan is a tough character. It was bad enough negotiating the terms of the contract with him!

'Don't get me wrong,' she said as Cassie's face fell. 'I'm delighted about the contract. But I'd hate to think you got hurt trying to save Avalon. I just think you should be careful about getting too involved with someone like that.'

'I'll be fine,' said Cassie buoyantly. 'Anyway, I'm not *involved* with Jake,' she said, firmly pushing the memory of last night's kiss away. 'Pretending to be engaged is simply a way to promote Portrevick Hall as a wedding venue. I'm just doing my job.'

She was still in a breezy mood when she rang Jake at his office later that morning.

'Hi!' she said when his PA put her through. 'It's me. Your brand-new fiancée,' she added, just in case he needed his memory jogging.

'Hello,' said Jake. He sounded cool and businesslike, and it was hard to believe that it was only a matter of hours since his lips had been warm and sure against hers.

'I think you mean "hello, *darling*", don't you?' Cassie prompted. 'We're engaged, remember?'

Jake sighed. 'Hello, *darling*,' he said ironically.

'OK, the darling is good, but you might want to work on your tone,' said Cassie, enjoying herself. 'You know? A bit lower, a bit warmer…a bit more like you're counting the seconds until you can see me again!'

'Darling,' Jake repeated obediently, and this time his voice was deep and warm and held a hint of a smile. Cassie's heart skipped just a little, even though she knew he was just pretending.

'Very good,' she approved.

'It's not that it's not wonderful to hear from you,' he said, reverting to his usual sardonic tone. 'But I've got a meeting in five minutes.'

'I won't keep you,' she promised. 'I just thought I'd tell you that I've spoken to *Wedding Belles* and broken the news that I'm the bride-to-be. I made up some story about being too shy to admit it before. I'm not sure if they believed me, but they're not asking too many questions, which is a relief.'

'Presumably they don't really care as long as they get a decent story.'

'Yes, that's right.' Cassie could feel his impatience to get off the phone. Just as well they weren't really engaged, or she *would* have been hurt. 'Anyway, we're committed now.'

'So what happens next?' asked Jake without much interest. Cassie imagined him scrolling through his emails while he listened to her with half an ear.

But she could do businesslike, too. 'I was just coming to that,' she said. 'It turns out that *Wedding Belles* is hosting a wedding fair at some fancy hotel this weekend. The opening party is on Friday night, and they want us to go. Apparently they're inviting all the couples who are going to be featured in the magazine next year, and we're getting a special preview of the show.'

She could practically see Jake grimacing at the idea. 'Do we have to go?'

'Yes, we do,' said Cassie briskly. 'This is the first part of the story. The photographer will be there, and we'll meet the editor, so we'll have to be on our best behaviour.

'Besides,' she said, 'the theme of the fair is Winter Wonderland Weddings, so we'll be able to pick up some ideas. Joss and I always go to the shows, but I've never been to the preview or the party before. It should be great.'

'What goes on at a wedding show?' Jake asked, not at all sure that he was going to like the answer.

'Oh, they're fantastic,' Cassie assured him. 'There's everything you could ever need to plan a wedding under one roof. It doesn't matter if you're looking for a chocolate fountain or a tiara: you'll find someone who specialises in providing just what you want for every stage of getting married, from the engagement party to the honeymoon. Oh, and there's always a fashion show too. We don't want to miss that.'

'A fashion show,' Jake echoed dryly. 'Fabulous!'

'It'll be fun,' Cassie told him.

Jake thought that it sounded as much fun as sticking pins in his eyes, but he was the one who had insisted that they go ahead with the article, so he could hardly quibble now.

Since the hotel was almost exactly halfway between their offices, they agreed to meet in the lobby at six-thirty on the Friday.

'OK, I'd better go,' said Cassie in the same brisk tone. About to switch off the phone, she paused. 'Oh, nearly forgot,' she said, and cooed, *'Love you!'* in an exaggeratedly saccharine voice before spoiling the effect by laughing.

Jake put the phone down and sat looking at it for a long moment, her gurgling laugh echoing in his ears. Then he smiled unwillingly, shook his head, and pushed back his chair to go to his meeting, where everyone would be sane and sensible and dressed in shades of grey.

* * *

Jake looked at his watch as Cassie came tumbling into the hotel's ornate lobby through the revolving door. 'You're late,' he said.

'I know, I know, I'm sorry,' she panted, struggling out of her coat. 'I spent all afternoon trying to track down a carriage for one of our clients. It wouldn't be a problem, except that she wants four horses—all white, naturally—and the carriage has to be purple to fit the colour theme. Oh, and did I mention she wants it for next weekend? I finally found someone who was prepared to paint the carriage, but by the time we'd negotiated how much it would all cost it was nearly six…'

Still talking, she managed to get rid of her coat and checked it into the cloakroom, which gave Jake a chance to get his breathing back under control. It had got ridiculously muddled up at the sight of Cassie spilling through the doors, her cheeks pink, her eyes bright and brown, and the wild curls even more tousled than usual. She was like a crisp autumn breeze, swirling into the stultifyingly grand lobby, freshening the air and sharpening his senses. For a moment there Jake had forgotten whether he was supposed to be breathing in or breathing out.

How had he come up with a crazy idea like pretending to be engaged to her? Jake had spent the day wondering if Giovanni's wine had gone to his head. It wasn't the plan that bothered him, it was Cassie. It was that aura of turbulence that always seemed to be whirling around her, that sense that everything might tip into chaos at any moment. Jake, whose life now was built on rigorous order and control, found it deeply unsettling.

If only she could be more like Natasha, who was always calm, always neat, always predictable.

Except when she was running off with Rupert, of course.

The memory of Rupert was enough to make Jake's jaw tighten with resolve. He might not like muddle and chaos, but he disliked Rupert more. He mustn't lose his nerve about the plan now, he told himself. It made perfect sense. Pretending to be engaged to Cassie would deprive Rupert of his triumph and achieve his most pressing objective, which was to get the Hall up and running. If a little pretence was required for the purposes of promotion, well, Jake could handle that.

It wasn't as if anyone in London would ever know anything about it, either, he reassured himself. No; everything would be fine.

It had been fine until that damned kiss.

Natasha's defection had been a blow to his pride, true, but he'd had a plan. Life had been back under control. And then Cassie had leant forward in the candlelight, that dimple deepening enticingly as she smiled. *Darling*, she had called him, and then she had kissed him.

The moment her lips had touched his, control had gone out the window. Jake had forgotten everything but warmth, softness and searing, seductive sweetness. He'd forgotten Rupert, forgotten Natasha, forgotten the *plan*.

It had taken him all day to remember what was important and get himself back under control, and all Cassie had had to do was appear and he'd lost it all over again.

He was being ridiculous, Jake told himself savagely. It was just Cassie. He looked at her as she tucked the cloakroom ticket away in her bag. She was wearing loose trousers and a fine-knit top with a wide belt. She looked really quite stylish for once, although nothing like as elegant as Natasha would have seemed in exactly the same outfit.

She was just a girl. Pretty, yes—in fact, much prettier than she seemed at first glance—but a bit messy, a bit clumsy, a bit disorganised. Nothing special, in fact. Not the kind of girl you got yourself into a state about, that was for sure.

CHAPTER SIX

'YOU'RE looking very fierce,' Cassie commented, hoisting her bag back onto her shoulder. 'You're supposed to be deliriously happy at the prospect of spending an evening with me planning our special day together!'

She saw his mouth turn down at the corners. 'Look, this was your idea,' she reminded him. 'The editor of *Wedding Belles* is going to be in there. If you want to promote the Hall, you're going to have to convince her the way you convinced me the other night.'

Jake raised his brows. 'What, I have to kiss her?'

'You're not taking this seriously,' said Cassie. 'All you've got to do is look affectionate and not as if you can't decide whether to fire me or shoot me!'

She was right, Jake thought. He was the one who had insisted on doing this. He bared his teeth in a smile. 'Better?'

'A bit,' she allowed, glancing around for signs to the wedding fair. A notice board pointed them down to the lower floor. 'Come on, then,' she said. 'Let's go and find the party.'

'Shouldn't we hold hands?' suggested Jake.

'Er, yes, we probably should. Good idea.'

Cassie tried to sound casual, but she was desperately aware of the dry warmth of his palm and the firm fingers closing around hers. He had lovely hands, big, strong and safe, the kind of hands that could catch you if you were falling, the kind of hands that wouldn't let you go.

She was being fanciful, Cassie told herself as they made their way downstairs, where they found the party already in full swing. She wasn't falling anywhere, not even off her heels, and Jake would be only too keen to let her go as soon as possible.

The editor of *Wedding Belles* was greeting arrivals at the door, but they managed to brush through the introductions without rousing any suspicions, and were disgorged into the party. A passing waiter offered them champagne and Cassie accepted thankfully. Holding Jake's hand was making her jittery and self-conscious, and it was the perfect excuse to drop it and grab a glass from the tray.

Amazing how a gulp of champagne could make you feel better, she thought, looking around her and trying not to notice how tingly and somehow empty her hand felt now. She switched the glass to give it something to hold.

'We'd better try and circulate,' she murmured.

They were standing next to another couple, who introduced themselves after a few banalities as Mark and Michelle; it soon turned out that it was Michelle who did all the talking.

'We're getting married in April,' she told Cassie and Jake. 'Aren't we, Mark?'

Mark opened his mouth to agree but she was already sweeping on. 'We've been planning the wedding for two years. We got engaged on a cruise, so our theme is the sea.'

'Theme?'

'The theme of the wedding.' Michelle looked at Jake as if he were stupid. 'Blue is our main colour, of course, so all our favours will be blue, and we're having blue sashes on the chair covers. We had waves on the invitations, didn't we, Mark? And we're naming all the tables after different seas,' she finished triumphantly.

'Who are you putting in the Bermuda Triangle?' asked Jake, and Cassie nudged him.

'That sounds lovely,' she said quickly. 'Have you decided on a dress yet?'

Michelle had, of course, and described it at length. Then she went on to tell them about their matching stationery, the wedding website, the special, blue fascinators she had sourced for her five bridesmaids, the first dance they were practising already, and the personalised shells that she was trying to track down as place settings.

Her monologue was punctuated with requests for confirmation from Mark, although the poor man never got a chance even to agree. Michelle had a spreadsheet she was using to keep track of her budget, and kept all the paperwork to do with the wedding in a colour-coded filing system.

Weddings were Cassie's business, and she wouldn't have minded listening to Michelle drone on if she hadn't been aware that Jake was glazing over beside her.

'We're having a Christmas wedding,' she interrupted brightly at last.

'I think you mean a Christmas *theme*, don't you?' muttered Jake.

'We're getting married this Christmas, actually,' Cassie hurried on, trying not to giggle.

'Really? So, not long to go!' Michelle looked from one to the other. 'You must be excited!'

'I'm beside myself,' Jake agreed, deadpan.

'Don't mind him,' said Cassie, taking his arm and leaning into him. 'He's thrilled, really—especially since we found him a Regency-buck outfit.' She smiled winsomely up at him. 'You're going to look *soooo* gorgeous in those breeches!'

She turned back to Michelle. 'We're going for the Mr Darcy look, you know? But he's worried he won't be able to tie his cravat properly.'

'I'm sure you can get instructions on the Internet,' said

Michelle, completely missing Jake's expression at the very thought of a cravat. 'So, are you going for a Regency dress as well?' she asked Cassie.

'I haven't got it yet,' Cassie admitted.

'You're getting married at Christmas and you haven't got your *dress*?' Michelle fell back in horror. 'You're leaving it very late!'

'Maybe I'll find something here tonight. Perhaps you're right; I could go for a period look and wear a bonnet.' She pretended to muse.

'A muff's very nice at a Christmas wedding,' offered Michelle.

That was when Cassie made the mistake of catching Jake's eye. 'Now, there's a thought,' he said, and waggled his eyebrows at her. It would have been fine if she hadn't just lifted her glass to her lips to hide her smile, and at that she spluttered champagne all down the front of her top and started choking.

Jake patted her none too gently on the back. 'Here, let's go and find you a glass of water,' he said, taking her by the arm and bearing her off with barely time for a goodbye to Michelle and the silent Mark.

'Look, my top is all stained,' Cassie complained, brushing champagne from her cleavage. 'And it's all your fault for making me laugh!'

'*My* fault? I wasn't the one who started on the Regency bucks!' said Jake. He had his hand on her back and was steering her firmly to the other side of the room. 'I couldn't stand it any longer. Poor Mark looked like he had lost the will to live, and I don't blame him. And what the hell is a "favour", anyway?'

'It's a little thank-you gift for your guests. It usually goes on the table as a memento of the day that they can take away.'

Jake snorted. 'Well, the only favour *I* want is for you to get me out of here!'

'We can't go yet,' said Cassie. 'We've only just arrived. Besides, they haven't opened the show. I think there are going to be some speeches first.'

Putting her empty glass down on a passing tray, she took another one and turned to see who else they could talk to. Fortunately, the next couple they met was less obsessed with weddings than Michelle. 'We're only here for the champagne,' Kevin said.

'And for the draw,' said Victoria. 'First prize is a weekend in Paris as a break from the stress of planning a wedding, but the others sound worth winning too. Everyone here tonight is in with a chance.'

'Paris sounds lovely,' Cassie said wistfully, imagining strolling around Montmartre hand in hand with Jake. Then she caught herself up. What was she thinking? They weren't lovers. There would be no one to see them in Paris. Why would they be holding hands?

She forced a smile. 'Not that I ever win anything. Oh, I take that back,' she said. 'I once won a jar of pickled onions in the tombola at the village fête.'

Victoria laughed. 'Well, it looks as if you've won yourself a gorgeous guy,' she said with a meaningful glance at Jake, who was talking to Kevin about a new sports channel.

'Yes,' said Cassie, stifling a little sigh.

'Isn't it the best feeling when you find the right guy?'

Cassie looked at Jake, deep in blokey conversation with Kevin. She remembered the feel of his hand holding hers, the devastating sureness of his lips. 'Yes,' she said in a hollow voice.

'I'd almost given up on men,' Victoria confided. 'I thought it was never going to happen for me. Then I walked into work one day, and there he was! The moment I saw him, I knew he was the one.'

She showed Cassie her engagement ring. 'Every time I look at it, I feel so happy I want to cry,' she said.

Kevin obviously caught the end of her sentence as he broke off his conversation with Jake. 'Oh no, not the "I'm so happy I could cry" line again?' he said, rolling his eyes, but he put his arm around Victoria and pulled her close. 'Do you get that one?' he asked Jake.

'Not yet,' said Jake.

There was a tiny pause, when it suddenly seemed glaringly obvious that they weren't touching with the easy affection Kevin and Victoria showed, but then he slid his hand beneath Cassie's hair and rested it at the nape of her neck.

'You don't want to cry, do you?'

Actually, right then, Cassie did. Her throat had tightened painfully, watching Victoria and Kevin so obviously in love, and now the warm, comforting weight of Jake's hand on her neck only made her eyes sting with tears. She blinked them firmly away and mustered a smile. 'I probably *would* cry with happiness if I had a lovely ring like Victoria's!' She pretended to joke.

'Hasn't he bought you a ring yet?' Victoria tutted.

'We haven't been engaged very long.' Cassie excused him, and then sucked in a breath as Jake caressed the nape of her neck.

'Besides,' he said. 'I'm waiting to find something really special for her.'

The more couples they talked to, the more wistful Cassie felt. The others were all so happy, so much in love, so excited about their weddings; the happier they were together, the more conscious she was that she and Jake were just pretending.

'Doesn't it make you feel a bit sad?' she asked him when they found themselves alone for a moment.

'Sad? No. Why?'

'Oh, I suppose I'm just envious,' she said with sigh. 'Everyone else here is in love, and we're just promoting the Hall.'

Over Jake's shoulder, she could see a couple laughing together. Unaware that anyone was watching them, the girl hugged her fiancé's arm and lifted her face naturally for his kiss. They looked so comfortable together that Cassie's heart twisted and she jerked her eyes back to Jake.

'It must be even worse for you,' she said, and he lifted his brows.

'For me?'

'You might have been here with Natasha,' Cassie said. 'It's never easy, seeing everyone else all loved up when your own relationship has just fallen apart.'

And she ought to know, she thought glumly. Her relationships had a nasty habit of crashing and burning after a few weeks, and she had almost given up on meeting someone she could fall in love with, someone who would love her back.

'I can't imagine Natasha here,' said Jake, looking around him with a derisive expression. 'We didn't have that kind of relationship. If we had decided to get married, she wouldn't have had much time for all of this.'

'All of what?'

'All this lovey-dovey stuff isn't a good basis for a strong marriage.'

He had given her that line before, Cassie remembered. She didn't buy it any more this time round. 'I would have thought love was the *only* real basis for a marriage,' she said.

'I don't agree with you,' said Jake coolly. 'Love is too random. It's a hit and miss affair, and even if you do get a hit it soon runs out of steam. How many times have you seen friends wild for their new partner, only to end up complaining about how they never put the top back on the toothpaste barely weeks later?'

All too often in her own case, thought Cassie.

'It doesn't always run out of steam,' she said. 'Sometimes it gets stronger. OK, the red-hot passion may not last, but it can change into something better, something that *will* last. When you love someone completely, you accept their little quirks as part of who they are. You certainly don't throw away a good relationship because they squeeze the toothpaste in the middle instead of rolling up the ends neatly!'

'Are you talking from your own experience?' asked Jake, and she lifted her chin.

'Not personally, no,' she said with dignity. 'But I've seen

plenty of other relationships where both partners learn to compromise because they love each other. It *can* work.'

'Not often enough.' Jake shook his head. 'Marriage is too serious a business to be left to love,' he said. 'It should be about shared interests, shared goals, about practicalities and the things that can't change. If you can add in sexual attraction as well, *then* you've got yourself a winning formula.'

'You can't reduce love to a formula, Jake.'

'What else is it?'

'It's—it's finding someone who makes your heart beat faster. Someone who makes your senses tingle.'

Hang on, that sounded alarmingly like the way Jake made her feel, Cassie realised uncomfortably.

'Someone who makes the sun shine brighter.' She hurried on into unfamiliar territory. Jake didn't do that, did he?

'That's just chemical attraction,' said Jake dismissively.

'It isn't chemistry that makes someone the first person you want to talk to in the morning and the last person you want to see at night,' Cassie said hotly. 'The person who believes in you, however bad things are, who will take you in their arms and make you feel that you've found a safe harbour.'

Her voice cracked a little. She had never found that person, but she wasn't giving up on the belief that he was out there somewhere, whatever Jake Trevelyan said. 'It's got nothing to do with chemistry,' she said, recovering.

'And how long does that feeling last?' Jake countered. He gestured around the room with his head. 'How many of these loving couples are going to feel like that a year from now, let alone in ten years, twenty years? Relying on how you feel is too random a way to choose a partner for life. Call it a formula, if you like, but if you're interested in the long haul you're better off sticking to what you know works.'

'The formula didn't work for you and Natasha, though, did it?' Cassie retorted without thinking.

There was a short, not entirely pleasant silence. 'No,' Jake said just as she opened her mouth to apologise. 'The formula isn't foolproof, sure. But if you find someone who fits your specifications I'd say your chances of a successful marriage are much greater than investing all your happiness in someone you don't really know.'

'Well,' said Cassie, draining her glass of champagne defiantly. 'I couldn't disagree with you more. It looks as if we're completely incompatible on that front, anyway. It's just as well we're not really getting married!'

'Just as well,' Jake agreed dryly.

At the front of the room, a microphone was spluttering into life. The editor of *Wedding Belles* was up on the little stage, making a speech and announcing the winners of the prize draw to much ooh-ing and aah-ing from the crowd. The happy couple who had won the trip to Paris was called up and had their photo taken, beaming from ear to ear.

It gave Cassie a chance to get a grip. There was a time, when they'd been chatting to other couples, when it had felt quite normal being with Jake. It had felt more than normal, in fact. It had felt strangely right to have him at her side, talking, laughing, being able to catch his eye and know that he would find the same comments amusing. For a while there, she had forgotten how different they were.

But the conversation just now had reminded her. Jake, it seemed, had a completely different idea of love. He was looking for someone who fitted his specifications the way Natasha had.

The way *she* never would. Cassie didn't need to ask what kind of woman Jake wanted. She was fairly sure the answer wouldn't be someone scatty, messy or with a poor time-keeping record. No, he would be looking for someone poised, quiet, elegant. Someone who would slot into the carefully controlled life he seemed to have built for himself since he'd left Portrevick.

And why is that a problem, Cassie?

It wasn't; Cassie answered her own question firmly. It wasn't as if she wanted a man like Jake either. Control freaks weren't her style. It didn't matter that they were completely incompatible. It wasn't as if they were actually having a relationship. This was just a pretence, and the less seriously they both took it the better.

Clutching their tickets to Paris, the winners of the first prize were leaving the stage, and more prizes were announced. Cassie was getting tired of clapping politely, and her thoughts were wandering so much that when she heard their own names called she hadn't even heard what they had won.

Perhaps her luck was changing at last, she thought buoyantly.

She dug Jake in the ribs with her elbow. 'Come on. We're on. Don't forget to smile!'

Together they climbed the stage; Cassie accepted a voucher from the editor, and they posed obediently for the camera.

'A bit closer,' called the photographer, and after the tiniest of hesitations Jake put his arm around Cassie, who had little choice but to snuggle in to his lean, hard body.

'Perfect,' said the photographer, and for a dangerous moment there it *felt* perfect too. Jake was warm and solid, and his arm was very strong. It felt wonderfully safe, being held hard against him, and Cassie found herself wishing that he would hold her like that for ever.

The moment the shot was taken, she straightened and pushed the treacherous thought aside, cross with herself. There was no point in thinking like that. Hadn't she just decided that they were incompatible?

'What have we won?' Jake asked out of the corner of his mouth as they left the stage and the next winners were called up.

Cassie opened the envelope and started to laugh. 'It's vouchers for a his 'n' hers day at a luxury spa, including treatments.'

'Treatments?' he asked nervously. 'What sort of treatments?'

'Oh, you know, pedicures, massages, waxing.'

Jake paled. '*Waxing*?'

'I believe a certain wax is very popular with men nowadays,' said Cassie naughtily, enjoying his expression of horror. 'You want to look your best for our wedding photos, don't you?'

'Not if it involves wax of any kind *anywhere*!'

'Oh well, if you're going to be such a baby…'

'Why don't we just give the voucher to someone else?'

'We can't do that. *Wedding Belles* might want photos of us enjoying our prize for the article.'

'If they think they're getting a photo of me having any hairs ripped out, they've got another think coming!' said Jake firmly.

'Don't worry; I'm sure we can find you something less painful,' Cassie soothed him as she flicked through the brochure that had come with the voucher. 'Maybe you could have a facial— or, I know, a seaweed wrap! That wouldn't hurt.'

Jake was looking aghast. 'A *wrap*?' Then he caught Cassie's dancing brown eyes, realised that she was teasing and relaxed into a laugh. 'If you *dare* book me in for anything like that, Cassie…!'

'What, and risk you cancelling our contract? No way— although it would be almost worth it to see your face.'

It was a good thing they had had that discussion about love earlier, Cassie decided. She had been in danger of forgetting that theirs wasn't a real relationship for a while, but now that she'd remembered she could relax and enjoy herself again.

She tucked her hand into his arm. 'Worry not,' she said. 'I wouldn't do anything like that to you.'

'So, can we go now?'

'Go? We haven't even started yet!' Cassie pointed to where a set of doors was swinging apart to revel a huge ballroom crammed with stalls. 'The show's just opened, and we've got a whole winter-wonderland of weddings to explore…'

'Have you got a moment?'

'Jake!' Cassie looked up in astonishment as he appeared

in the doorway. It was the following Tuesday, and she was sitting on the office floor surrounded by fabric samples. She scrambled to her feet, ridiculously breathless. 'What on earth are you doing here?'

He was looking uncharacteristically hesitant. 'I wanted to ask a favour. In the circumstances, it seemed only fair that I should come to you, but I can go away if you're busy.'

'No, no. It's fine.' Cassie swept a pile of magazines off a chair. 'Sit down. I'm sorry it's all such a mess.'

She grimaced, looking at the office through Jake's eyes. They really ought to tidy up some time. Every surface was piled high with magazines, fabric books, photographs, brochures, and samples of everything you could think of from thank-you cards to lip salves to artificial flowers. A wedding dress in a protective bag hung from a door, and the walls were covered with photos of all the weddings Avalon had planned. It was a colourful, cheerfully chaotic place, but, coming from his immaculately cool and contemporary office, Jake was unlikely to be impressed.

'Coffee?' she offered, and then wished she hadn't. They only had chipped mugs, and the milk was probably off.

'No. Thank you.'

Phew. Cassie lifted a pile of cake-design brochures off another chair and sat down. A favour, he had said. 'So, what can I do for you?'

She was rather proud of how normal she sounded, not at all as if her heart was bouncing around in her ribcage and interfering ludicrously with her breathing. She was disconcerted, in fact, by how pleased she was to see Jake.

In the end, they had had a good time at the wedding fair, and the weekend had seemed, well, a bit *empty* without him. Jake had said goodnight as they parted, but hadn't mentioned meeting again. Why would he? It was her job to get things going at the Hall, and she had that well in hand. They would need to arrange a photo session at some point, but the Hall wasn't ready for that yet.

As it was, the week stretched drearily ahead. Cassie had even caught herself wondering if she could invent an excuse to call him, and had had to give herself a stern talking-to, reminding herself about key words like 'contract', 'professionalism', and 'incompatibility'.

Jake seemed to be having trouble deciding where to start. 'Remember that voucher we won on Friday?' he said at last.

He had taken so long that Cassie had begun to worry that he was about to give her bad news. Relief made her laugh. 'Look, there's no need to worry,' she assured him, relaxing. 'I won't book anything.'

'It's not that.' Jake wanted to get to his feet, but the office was so crowded with stuff that there was nowhere to step, let alone pace. How on earth did Cassie manage to work in all this clutter?

He brought his attention back to the matter in hand. 'It turns out that one of the accountants at Primordia is getting married next year, and she was at the *Wedding Belles* party.'

'Ah,' said Cassie, seeing where this was going at last.

'I didn't recognise her, but she thought she recognised me, apparently, and when our names were announced as winners of that bloody voucher that just confirmed it. So she trotted in to work yesterday and mentioned to someone she worked with in finance that I was engaged.'

'And word went round faster than you can say "seaweed wrap"?'

Jake nodded heavily. 'That's about it. The next thing I know, Ruth, my communications director, is congratulating me and saying I must bring you to some fund-raising event we're sponsoring on Thursday.' He sighed. 'I can't believe how quickly it's all got out of hand. I didn't think anyone in London would need to know about our so-called engagement,' he confessed. 'I obviously didn't think things through properly.'

'You weren't to know anyone from work would be at the wedding fair,' Cassie pointed out consolingly.

'No.' Jake brooded, trying to work out where it had all gone wrong. He wasn't used to his plans going awry. He spent so much of his life keeping things under rigid control; this was way out of his comfort zone.

'Perhaps I should have laughed it off when Ruth first mentioned it,' he said. 'But it seemed humiliating to admit that my engagement was just a marketing exercise. Ruth knew Natasha, too. She would have felt sorry for me.'

He didn't need to tell Cassie how much he would have hated that.

'The upshot is that I let her believe that you and I really were engaged,' he went on, looking directly at Cassie. 'I'm sorry about this, but I wondered if you would mind putting on an appearance at this do on Thursday, and any other similar events in the next couple of months?' He took a breath. 'If you don't want to do it, I'll understand, of course.'

'What, no more blackmail?' said Cassie, brown eyes dancing.

Jake set his teeth. 'No. This wasn't part of our agreement. I'm just asking you to help me.'

'Of course I will,' said Cassie, regretting now that she'd teased him. He so obviously hated the whole situation. 'It'll be fine. Honestly, I don't mind.'

'It's not likely to be a big deal,' Jake said. 'Just a couple of outings.'

'There you go, then. No problem.'

'Well…thank you.'

Jake was taken aback by how relieved he was, and he had a nasty feeling it wasn't just because Cassie was prepared to save his face at work. It was barely two weeks since she had—literally—tripped back into his life, and already she had changed things more than Natasha had in six months.

That wedding fair on Friday…Jake had thought about it all weekend. Cassie had dragged him round every stall. She had tried on tiaras and sampled cupcakes. She had sighed over shoes and chatted to other brides-to-be about make-up and hen parties and how to keep children entertained at a reception.

It should have been Jake's worst nightmare, but oddly he'd found that he was enjoying himself. He'd liked watching Cassie's animated face as she talked and waved her arms around, her intent expression as she'd studied the dizzying array of goods and services on offer, and the way she'd licked her fingers after trying a piece of fruit at the chocolate fountain.

They had wrangled over table decorations, pretended to choose a honeymoon destination, dodged behind stalls to avoid Michelle and the ever-silent Mark, and generally laughed more than Jake could remember since... Well, he couldn't remember the last time he had laughed like that. And all the time he had been aware of Cassie, of her bright face and her warm smile, and the memory of her kiss was like a hum underneath his skin.

So when Ruth had congratulated him on his engagement, instead of quietly admitting that it was all a mistake he had imagined seeing Cassie again, and he had found himself playing along.

It was only after Ruth had gone that he'd realised how much he had taken it for granted that Cassie would agree. He had blackmailed her into this charade, for goodness' sake! That didn't happen to nice middle-class girls like her. Jake wouldn't have blamed her if she had told him to stuff his pretence.

After all, it wasn't as if she could like being with him. They'd got on well enough at the wedding fair, but in lots of ways being there had just pointed out the differences between them. Cassie was ridiculously romantic, he was rigidly practical. She was warm, vibrant and spontaneous, he was cool and controlled. The only thing they could agree on was that they were completely incompatible.

Jake had told himself he would deserve the humiliation of admitting to Ruth that he had lied if Cassie didn't agree.

But she had agreed. 'It'll be fine,' she had said easily, and Jake had felt his heart lift.

'Thank you,' he said again.

'When do you want me?'

Now. I want you now. Unbidden, the words hovered on the tip of Jake's tongue. He clamped his lips together, aghast at how close he had come to opening his mouth and letting them spill out without any idea of where the thought had come from.

Cassie misunderstood his silence. A blush unfurled in her cheeks. 'On Thursday, I mean.'

'Can you come to my office at six?' said Jake, recovering. 'The reception starts at half past. We may as well go together and look like a proper couple.'

CHAPTER SEVEN

'DON'T say anything!' Unbuttoning her coat, Cassie collapsed onto one of the sofas in Jake's office. 'I was so determined I was going to be on time for once, but it's really not my fault this time,' she told him. 'I've been stuck on the tube for *forty* minutes!' She groaned at the memory. 'Some problem with the signals, they said. I thought I was never going to get here.'

Jake didn't sit down. He needed a few moments to readjust. Had he actually been worrying about her? He had certainly started looking at his watch a good half-hour before she was even due to arrive, and as the minutes ticked past six o'clock he had looked more and more frequently.

And now she was here, lying on the sofa in a pose of exaggerated exhaustion, looking extraordinarily vivid. Her coat had fallen open to reveal a party dress. Jake had an impression of a vibrant blue colour, and some kind of satiny material, but all he really noticed was that it was rucked up over Cassie's knees, and in spite of himself his eyes travelled over the legs sprawled over the leather. His mouth dried. Had Cassie always had those spectacular legs? Surely he would have noticed if she had?

Clearing his throat, Jake made himself look away. 'If you're too tired, we can always give the party a miss.'

'Absolutely not.' Cassie sat up. 'How can we convince everyone we're engaged if we don't turn up? I'm fine,' she said, pushing back her hair.

Getting to her feet, she crossed to the window, and looked down at the street below. The traffic was nose to tail, the pavements choked with umbrellas, everyone anxious to get home or heading for the nearest pub. Thousands of people, all with somewhere to go and something to do, even in the rain. She loved London like this, busy, purposeful and pulsating with energy.

Jake was reaching for his coat when he stopped. 'Oh, I nearly forgot...' He patted his jacket and pulled a small jewellery-box from the inside pocket. 'You'd better have this.'

Cassie turned from window. 'What is it?'

'Open it.'

Jake handed the box to Cassie, who opened it almost fearfully and found herself staring down at a ring set with three large square-cut rubies separated by two dazzling diamonds.

'Oh...' she said on a long breath.

Watching her face, Jake found himself rushing into speech. 'I remembered how all the other brides at the wedding fair had a ring,' he said. 'I thought you needed one for tonight. It would be odd if we'd got as far as announcing our engagement and you didn't have one. Do you like it?' he finished abruptly.

Cassie raised her eyes from the ring to look directly into his, and Jake felt as if a great fist was squeezing his heart. 'It's beautiful,' she said.

'Perhaps I should have gone down on one knee.' He tried to joke in a weak attempt to disguise his relief. He didn't want to admit even to himself how long he had spent choosing the damn thing, or how determined he had been to find exactly the right ring for her.

The brown eyes flickered and dropped again to the ring. 'There's no need for that,' she said. 'It's just a prop.'

A prop he had spent a whole afternoon agonising over. 'Yes,' said Jake.

Cassie pulled the ring out of the velvet and slipped it onto her finger. She couldn't help imagining what it would have been like if this was a real engagement ring, if Jake had bought it for her because he loved her.

She swallowed the tightness from her throat. 'It's really lovely,' she told him. 'It must have been terribly expensive. Will you be able to take it back when this is all over?' she said, just to reassure him that she hadn't forgotten that they were just pretending.

Jake was shrugging himself into his coat. 'I expect so,' he said.

'I'll take great care of it,' Cassie promised, overwhelmed by the feel of the ring on her finger.

She had never worn anything remotely as beautiful or as valuable, and the thought that Jake had chosen it for her made the breath snare again in her throat. He could have picked out a plain diamond, which would have done the job just as well, but instead he had bought *this*.

'It's gorgeous,' she said, turning her hand so that the gems flashed in the light. 'Look what a beautiful warm glow it has.'

Jake didn't need to look. The glowing warmth was the reason he had bought the ring. It had reminded him of her.

'Does it fit?' he asked.

'It's a tiny bit loose, maybe,' said Cassie, turning the ring on her finger. 'But it'll be fine just for a couple of evenings. How on earth did you know what size to get?'

'One of the assistants in the shop had hands about the same size as yours.'

Cassie didn't think Jake had ever noticed her hands. The thought that he had felt like a tiny shiver deep inside her.

'Well…thank you,' she said.

An awkward silence fell. If it had been anyone else, Cassie wouldn't have hesitated to kiss him. Just on the cheek, of course; it was the obvious way to thank him for choosing such a lovely ring for her to wear, even if only temporarily.

But Jake had stepped back after giving her the box, and now he wasn't close enough for her to give him a quick hug or brush her cheek against his. She would have had to walk across to him, and that would have made too much of a big deal of it, wouldn't it? It wasn't as if he had given her the ring because he loved her. He had agreed that it was just a prop.

Jake put an end to her dithering by looking at his watch. 'We'd better go,' he said. 'We're late.'

Outside, it was still raining. The tyres of the passing cars hissed on the wet tarmac, and the pavements gleamed with puddles. Cassie huddled into her coat. It was only the middle of September, but the temperature had dropped over the last few days, and there was an unmistakable smell of autumn in the air.

'Where are we going?' she asked.

'The Strand,' said Jake, and her face fell.

'That's miles!'

'It's too far for you to walk in those shoes, certainly,' he said, nodding down at them.

'What shall we do? We'll never get a taxi in this weather.'

The words were barely out of Cassie's mouth when Jake put two fingers in his mouth and produced a piercing whistle that had a taxi heading in the opposite direction, turning instantly and ignoring the blare of horns to cut right across the traffic and pull up in front of them.

'Well, that was annoying,' said Cassie as Jake opened the door with a mocking bow. 'But a relief too,' she decided, sinking back into the seat and fastening her seatbelt.

'The Savoy,' Jake told the taxi driver, and sat back beside her. 'Why don't you wear something more sensible on your feet?' he said, half-relieved to find something to irritate him again. He scowled at her shoes. 'Look at them—they're ridiculous!'

'They're not ridiculous!' Stung, Cassie stuck her legs straight out in front of her so she could admire her shoes. Perhaps the heels weren't *that* practical, but she loved the sling backs, and the cute, peep-toe effect, and the hot pink was a fabulous colour. 'They're party shoes. I couldn't wear sensible shoes with a party dress, now, could I? That really *would* be ridiculous!'

Jake wished she'd put her legs down. They were distracting him. *She* was distracting him.

He had to keep reminding himself that this was Cassie. He'd known her as an eager child, as an ungainly adolescent. She had never been cool, clever or graceful, or any of the things he admired in a girl. She was an unstable force, chaotic and uncontrollable.

And now that force was bouncing uncontrollably around in his carefully constructed life.

Jake didn't like it one little bit. He had spent ten years fighting his way to the top, ten years making sure he never had to go back to Portrevick. He had changed himself quite deliberately. He had had enough of being the child wearing cast-offs, the troublemaker, the one who made eyebrows twitch suspiciously whenever he walked along the street. He had made himself cool, focused, guarded. Invulnerable.

Until Rupert Branscombe Fox had cracked his defences by taking Natasha from him, and Cassie had kicked them down completely the moment she'd laid her mouth against his.

Dragging his eyes from Cassie's legs, Jake made himself look out of the window. They were driving along the Embankment, and the Thames gleamed grey and oily in the rain, but he didn't see the river. He saw Cassie—her eyes dark and glowing in candlelight. Cassie perched on the table at Portrevick Hall, swinging her legs. Cassie laughing as she tried on a fancy tiara. Cassie looking down at the ring on her finger.

He was disturbingly aware of her warm, bright presence on the other side of the taxi. Her perfume was already achingly familiar. When had that happened? His careful life seemed to be unravelling by the minute, and Jake didn't like the feeling at all.

Completely unaware of the desperate trend of his thoughts, Cassie was patting her hair, trying to smooth it into some kind of shape. Jake's hands itched to do it for her, to slide into the soft curls, the way they had in the restaurant before that buffoon Giovanni had interrupted them. He imagined twisting its silkiness around his fingers, tucking it neatly behind her delicate ears, and then he could let his hands drift down her throat, let his lips follow…

'Is this it?' said Cassie, leaning forward to peer through the window as the taxi drew up outside the hotel, and Jake had to unscramble his thoughts enough to pay the taxi driver.

At least he had a few minutes to pull himself together while Cassie disappeared into a cloakroom to leave her coat and check her make-up. Adjusting the knot of his tie, he made himself think of something other than Cassie and the strange, disturbing way she made him feel. He remembered Portrevick instead, and the grim house where he had grown up. That was always a good way to remind himself of the importance of control. He thought about his mother's worn face, and the long, silent bus rides to visit his father in prison.

And then he thought about Rupert's supercilious smile and his jaw tightened. If it wasn't for Rupert, he wouldn't be in this mess. If it wasn't for Rupert, he and Natasha could have posed for a few photographs for this damned article and that would have been that. If it wasn't for Rupert, he would never have kissed Cassie, and he wouldn't be standing here now, unable to shake the feel of her, the taste of her, the scent of her from his mind.

Jake gave his tie a final wrench and looked at his watch. What the hell was Cassie doing in there? He was just getting ready to storm into the Ladies and drag her out when she appeared, smoothing down her dress. It was short and simply cut, and held up with tiny spaghetti-straps that left her shoulders bare. The colour—less a blue than a purple, he could see now—was so vivid that it dazzled the eye—or maybe that was just Cassie, Jake thought as the breath leaked from his lungs. She looked warm, lush, bright and unbelievably sexy. As she walked towards him he couldn't help remembering another time, ten years ago, when she had walked towards him in a different dress.

Cassie was smiling as she walked towards him, but as she got closer and her eyes met that dark, deep-blue gaze she faltered and the smile evaporated from her face. All at once, the air seemed to close around them, sealing them into an invisible bubble and sucking the air out of her lungs. The babble and laughter from Reception inside the big doors faded, and there was just Jake, watching her with unfathomable eyes, and a silence that stretched and twanged with the memory of how it had felt to kiss him.

Suddenly ridiculously shy, she struggled to think of something to say. Something other than 'kiss me again', anyway. 'How do I look?' was the best she could do.

'Very nice,' said Jake.

He couldn't have said anything better to break the tension, thought Cassie gratefully. 'No,' she told him, rolling her eyes. 'Not "very nice". You're in love with me, remember? Tell me I look beautiful or gorgeous or sexy—anything but *very nice*!'

'Maybe I won't say anything at all,' said Jake. 'Maybe I'll just do this instead.' And, putting his hands to her waist, he drew her to him and kissed her.

His lips were warm and persuasive, and wickedly exciting. Afterwards, Cassie thought that she should have resisted somehow, but at the time it felt so utterly natural that she melted into him without even a token protest. Her hands spread over his broad chest, and she parted her lips with a tiny murmur low in her throat.

It wasn't a long kiss, but it was a very thorough one, and Cassie's knees were weak when Jake let her go.

'Sometimes actions speak louder than words,' he said.

From somewhere, Cassie produced a smile. It felt a little unsteady, but at least it was a smile. At least she could pretend that her heart wasn't thudding, that her bones hadn't dissolved, and that her arms weren't aching to cling to him. That she didn't desperately, desperately want him to kiss her again.

'That's better,' she said, astonished at how steady her voice sounded. 'See how convincing you can be when you try?'

'Let's hope we can convince everyone else too,' said Jake. 'Ready?'

Of course she wasn't ready! How could he kiss her like that and then expect her to calmly swan into a party and act like a chief executive's fiancée—whatever one of those was like?

But she had agreed, and to make some feeble excuse now would just make it look as if she had been thrown into confusion by a meaningless kiss. Even if she had, Cassie didn't want Jake to know it.

She drew a deep breath. 'Ready,' she said.

Jake kept a hand at the small of her back as they made their way through the crowd. Cassie was intensely aware of it, and even when he dropped his arm she could feel its warmth like a tingling imprint on her skin burnt through the fabric of her dress.

She was nervous at first, but Jake seemed to know a lot of people there, and everyone was very friendly. There was quite a bit of interest when he introduced her as his fiancée, and Cassie wondered how many of them had known Natasha. It soon became clear, in fact, that they should have prepared their story more carefully.

'So, where did you pop up from, Cassie?' someone asked, and Jake put an arm around her waist.

'We knew each other years ago,' he said. 'We met up again recently.'

'Oh, so you've found your first love again? How sweet!'

'Well, not really,' said Jake, just as Cassie said,

'Yes. Jake was the first boy who ever kissed me.'

There was a tiny silence. 'Jake wasn't in love with me.' Cassie rose to the occasion magnificently. 'But I had a thing about him for years. Didn't I?' she said to Jake, but he was looking so baffled that she swept on, feeling rather like Michelle at the wedding fair. 'Anyway, the moment we met up again, it just clicked.'

She chattered on, inventing an entire love-affair while Jake watched her distractedly. He had been completely thrown by that kiss out there in the lobby. What had possessed him to kiss her like that? But she had looked so warm and enticing, he couldn't help himself. Now he could still taste the soft lips that had parted in surprise, still feel her body melting into his.

As the party wore on, Jake was achingly aware of Cassie by his side, a vibrant, glowing figure chatting animatedly to whoever they met. She was behaving beautifully—much better than him, anyway, Jake thought. *Look at her*, showing off her ring, turning a laughing face to his, leaning into him as if it was the most natural thing in the world for her to be here with him.

It was obvious that everyone found her so charming that Jake began to feel almost resentful. He didn't want Cassie to be able to play her role so well. He wanted her to be as disconcerted by him as he was by her.

She seemed to be managing perfectly well on her own, so he joined a neighbouring group in the hope that a little distance would help. But it was almost impossible to concentrate on chit-chat when he could feel Cassie somewhere behind him, not touching him, not talking to him, not even looking at him, but her presence as immediate as if she had laid a hand against his bare skin.

Jake finished his champagne in a gulp and looked around for a fresh glass, only to find himself face to face with the two people he least wanted to see. They saw him at the same time. Natasha looked appalled, Rupert predictably amused.

'Well, well, look who's here,' said Rupert. 'We'd no idea you'd be here too, Jake—but it's inevitable we had to meet some time, I suppose. Much best to get the first meeting over in civilised surroundings, I can't help feeling. After all, we're a little old for pistols at dawn, don't you think?'

Jake ignored that. 'Rupert,' he acknowledged him curtly. 'And Natasha.' It was odd, he thought, how much of a stranger she seemed already. 'How are you?'

'I'm fine,' she said, but Jake didn't think that she was looking her best. She was still beautiful, of course, but after Cassie she seemed a bit muted. She had none of Cassie's vitality, none of her warmth. It was hard to remember now how bitter he had felt at losing her.

Rupert put his arm around her. 'We've just been talking about getting married, haven't we, darling?' The question was for Natasha, but the words were aimed squarely at Jake. Rupert's smile was slyly triumphant. 'It's an awkward situation, knowing how much Natasha meant to you, but we hope you'll be pleased for us.'

'Or are you just hoping that I'll end the trust?' Jake asked.

'I believe marriage to a sensible woman *was* the condition—and Natasha is certainly that, aren't you, sweetheart?'

'Settling down was also a condition,' said Jake. 'When you've been married a year or so, I'll consider it.'

There was an unpleasant silence. Jake and Rupert eyed each other with acute dislike, and Jake found himself longing for Cassie. He could hardly go and drag her away from the conversation she was having just because he was confronting Rupert and Natasha on his own.

But suddenly there she was anyway, almost as if she'd sensed that he needed her, touching his rigid back, tucking her hand into his arm. Jake felt something unlock inside his chest.

Cassie studied Natasha. She was very lovely, with immaculate, silvery-blonde hair, green eyes, flawless skin, and intimidatingly well-groomed. From her perfect eyebrows to the tips of her beautifully manicured nails, Natasha was a model of elegance and restraint. She was wearing a simple top and silk trousers, but the combination of subdued neutrals and striking jewellery was wonderful.

'Classy' was the only word Cassie could think of to describe her, and her heart sank. Next to Natasha, she felt like a garish lump.

Why hadn't she thought to wear black or elegant neutral

colours like every other woman here? Cassie wondered miserably. She should have known this would be a sophisticated party. She looked ludicrously out of place in her vivid, purple dress and pink shoes. No wonder Jake had been distracted since they'd come in. He must be horribly embarrassed by her. He was used to being with Natasha, who fitted into this world in a way she never could.

How awful for Jake, to come face to face with the woman he loved on the arm of a man he hated, and to realise just what he had lost. Cassie had sensed his sudden tension somehow, and had turned to see him with Rupert and a woman she had known instantly was Natasha. His shoulders were set rigidly, and his back when she had touched it to let him know that she was there had been as stiff and as unyielding as a plank.

Well, she might not be Natasha, but she was here, and she could help him through this awkward meeting if nothing else.

Forcing a smile, Cassie turned her attention to Rupert. Even if she hadn't seen his photo in the papers over the years, she would have recognised him. He was still astonishingly good-looking, with golden hair, chiselled features and mesmerising blue eyes. It was only when you looked a little closer that you could see the lines of dissipation around his eyes.

And the faint bump in his nose where it had been broken. Cassie hoped Jake could see it, too.

'Hello, Rupert,' she said pleasantly.

Rupert looked at her, arrested. 'Do we know each other?'

'We used to,' said Cassie. 'Portrevick?' she prompted him. 'Cassie Grey? My father was Sir Ian's estate manager.'

'Good God, *Cassie*! I do remember now, but I would never have recognised you.' Rupert's eyes ran over her appreciatively. 'Well, well, well,' he drawled, evidently remembering how she had looked the last time he'd seen her. 'Who would have thought it? You look absolutely gorgeous! How lovely to see you, darling.' Taking his arm from around Natasha, he kissed her warmly on both cheeks.

The force of his charm was hard to resist, but Cassie felt Jake stiffen, and she made herself step back. 'How are you, Rupert?'

'All the better for seeing you,' he said, eyeing her with lazy appreciation. 'Where have you been hiding yourself all these years?'

How odd, thought Cassie. Here she was with Rupert, who hadn't recognised her, and was doing a very good impression of being bowled over by her looks. It was just like her fantasy.

But in her fantasy she hadn't been aware of Jake beside her, dark and rigid with hostility. She could see a muscle twitching in his jaw. He must be hating this.

'Growing up,' she said, and for the first time realised that it was true. She could look at Rupert and see that he was just a handsome face, a teenage fantasy, but not a man you could ever build a real relationship with. Had Natasha come to realise that as well? Cassie wondered. It seemed to her that the other woman's eyes were on Jake rather than Rupert, and when Cassie took Jake's hand Natasha's gaze sharpened unmistakably.

Jake's fingers closed hard around hers. 'Cassie, this is Natasha.' He introduced her stiffly.

Natasha smiled, although it looked as if it was a bit of an effort. 'You've obviously met before,' she said.

'We all grew up together in Cornwall,' said Cassie cheerfully. 'I was madly in love with Rupert for years.' She laughed. 'You know how intense adolescent love is? I promise you, I adored him.'

'You mean you don't any more?' said Rupert with mock disappointment, and with one of his patented smiles guaranteed to make a girl go weak at the knees.

Ten years ago, Cassie would have dissolved in a puddle at a smile like that. This time her knees stayed strangely steady. 'Not since I discovered what real love is,' she said, smiling at Jake, who looked straight back into her eyes; for a second the two of them were quite alone.

And then her knees *did* wobble.

Rupert's brows shot up. 'You and Jake…? How very unlikely!' His voice was light and mocking, but Cassie refused to be fazed.

'That's what we thought, didn't we, darling?' she said to Jake, and to her relief he managed to unclench his jaw at last.

'We thought we were completely different,' he agreed. 'And it turns out that we are made for each other.'

'What do your parents think about that?' Rupert asked Cassie smoothly. 'The Greys and the Trevelyans used to move in rather different social circles, as I remember.'

Cassie lifted her chin. 'They're delighted,' she told him. 'They're coming back to Portrevick for the wedding,' she added, and heard Natasha's sharp intake of breath.

'Wedding?'

'We're getting married at Christmas.' Cassie held out her hand to show her the ring, and then wished she hadn't. Her nail polish was bright-pink and chipped, and looked slatternly compared to Natasha's perfect French manicure. She pulled her hand back quickly.

'Engaged?' said Rupert. 'That's very sudden, isn't it?'

'It must seem that way to other people,' said Cassie, annoyed by his mocking expression. Anyone would think he didn't believe them. 'But to me it feels as if I've been waiting all my life to find Jake again.'

Slipping an arm around his waist, she leant adoringly into him. 'I can't believe how lucky I am. I always thought about him, but I never dreamt we would bump into each other again, and as soon as we did…bang! That was it, wasn't it, darling?'

'It was,' said Jake. 'It's enough to make you believe in fate. Cassie came along just when I needed her. I should thank you,' he said to Rupert and Natasha. 'I didn't think so at the time, I must admit, but you both did me a huge favour. If it hadn't been for you, I might never have found Cassie again.'

'So pleased to have been of help,' said Rupert a little tightly.

Natasha managed a bleak smile. 'Christmas is very soon.

I thought you didn't believe in rushing into things,' she said to Jake.

'I didn't until I met Cassie. But I know I want to spend the rest of my life with her, so there doesn't seem much point in waiting.'

Cassie saw the stricken look in Natasha's eyes and for a moment felt sorry for her. But only for a moment. Natasha had hurt Jake. She had left him for Rupert, but it was clear she wasn't at all happy to see him with someone else. It wouldn't do her any harm to think about just what she had thrown away, Cassie decided.

'It's going to be a bit of a rush to get everything organised in time,' she said, with another adoring look at Jake. 'But you're all for it, aren't you?'

'Absolutely,' he said, and a smile creased his eyes as he looked back at her. 'I'm just worried about where I'm going to get that Regency-buck outfit.'

'Regency buck?' echoed Rupert with a contemptuous look as Cassie smothered a giggle, and Jake met his eyes squarely.

'Cassie has always had a Mr Darcy fantasy. If she wants me in a cravat, I'll wear one,' he lied. 'Actually, Rupert, you might be able to give me a few tips about how to wear one. You look like the kind of man who knows his way around a cravat.'

Rupert's eyes narrowed dangerously. Clearly he couldn't decide whether Jake was joking about what he was wearing, but he knew a snide attack when he heard one. 'I'm afraid not, old chap,' he said. 'Natasha, there's Fiona—didn't you want to have a word with her? We'd better move on. Congratulations, and it was *marvellous* to see you again, Cassie.'

He produced a card as if by magic and handed it to her, as Natasha nodded to them both and headed off as if grateful to escape. 'We should meet up and talk about old times,' he said caressingly in her ear as he kissed her goodbye. 'I know Jake works all hours, but, as you're so in love, I'm sure he trusts you off the leash! Why don't you give me a ring some time?'

Cassie looked after him, fingering the card. By rights she should have been thrilled. Rupert Branscombe Fox wanted her to ring him! He was as devastatingly attractive as ever, but she couldn't shake the feeling that he had only shown an interest in her to rile Jake. Years ago, Jake had pointed out that Rupert was only interested in girls who belonged to someone else, and it seemed as if he hadn't changed very much. He had taken Natasha from Jake. Did he really think he could seduce her away, too?

She glanced at Jake, who was wearing a shuttered expression. 'Don't worry,' she said, 'I'm not going to ring him.'

His face closed even further. 'It's up to you,' he said abruptly. 'We're not really engaged. Keep the card, and you can call Rupert when all this is over.'

Cassie stared at him, hurt. She had forgotten about the pretence for a while, but clearly Jake hadn't. Then she remembered how difficult it must have been for him to pretend, with Natasha looking so beautiful with Rupert, and she felt guilty for not realising how embarrassing it would be for him if he suspected that there was a danger of her taking this all too seriously.

She tucked the card away in her bag. 'Maybe I will,' she said.

CHAPTER EIGHT

'IT'S coming on well, isn't it?' Cassie watched anxiously as Jake looked around the great hall. She badly wanted him to be impressed with the progress they had made, but to his eyes it must still look a bit of a mess.

'That scaffolding will come down as soon as the decorators have finished that last bit of ceiling,' she said. 'And then the sheets will come up so you can see the floor. That still needs to be cleaned, but the fireplace and the windows have been done—see?—and they've made a good start on the panelling, too.'

Cassie had a nasty feeling that she was babbling, but she was feeling ridiculously nervous. This was the first time she'd seen Jake since the reception at the Savoy. It had been a busy couple of weeks, most of which she had spent running up and down between London and Portrevick so that she could keep an eye on the work at the Hall. But there had still been rather too much time to think about Jake and remember how it had felt when he had kissed her.

To wonder if he would ever kiss her again.

Not that there seemed much chance of that. Jake hadn't asked her to appear as his fiancée again. She had obviously been much too crass. Cassie felt hot all over whenever she thought about how garish she had looked that evening. She must have stuck out like a tart at a vicar's tea-party. It wasn't surprising that Jake wasn't keen to repeat the experience. He only had to look at her next to Natasha's immaculate elegance to realise just how unconvincing a fiancée she made.

Their only contact since then had been by email. Cassie sent long, chatty messages about what was happening at the Hall, and Jake sent terse acknowledgements. She couldn't help wishing that he would show a little more interest. Email was convenient, but she wanted to hear his voice. She needed to know what he thought about the decisions she was making. It was lonely doing it all on her own.

But that was what he was paying her for, Cassie had to keep reminding herself. What was the point in a consultant you had to encourage the whole time, after all? Still, she had thought that they had more than a strictly businesslike relationship. They had laughed together. They had pretended to be in love.

They had *kissed*.

Whenever she thought about those kisses—and it was far too often—Cassie's heart would start to slam against her ribs. The memory of Jake's mouth—the feel of it, the taste of it— uncoiled like a serpent inside her, shivering along her veins and stirring up her blood.

It was stupid.

It was embarrassing.

It was pointless.

Time and again, Cassie reminded herself that Jake only cared about saving face with Rupert. The engagement was a tactic, that was all, one that had the added advantage of promoting the Hall so that he could rid himself of an unwanted responsibility. He hated Portrevick and all it represented. Once the Hall was up and running as a wedding venue, he would settle their fee and that would be that. She had to keep things strictly professional.

That didn't stop her heart lurching whenever she saw an email from him in her inbox, or sinking just a little when she read the brief message. It didn't stop her hoping that he would come down at the weekend, or being ridiculously disappointed when he decided to stay in London instead.

But he was here now. Cassie had—rather cleverly, she thought—arranged with *Wedding Belles* that they would supply photos themselves rather than have the magazine send a photographer all the way from London to Cornwall. It would be cheaper for the magazine, and much more convenient for them.

Tina's boyfriend was a photographer, Cassie had explained to Jake in one of her many emails. He and Tina were in on the secret, and Cassie had organised for him to take some photographs to illustrate the article. They needed some shots of the two of them apparently working on the renovation of the Hall and preparing for the wedding together, Cassie had told Jake. Could he come to Cornwall that weekend?

He would come down on Saturday, Jake had agreed, and Cassie had been jittery all day while she'd waited for him to arrive. She had changed three times that morning, and hours before there was any chance that he would turn up she would jump every time she heard a car. It was impossible to concentrate on anything, and even the most prosaic of conversations had her trailing off in mid-sentence or unable to make a decision about whether she wanted a cup of tea or not.

'What on earth is the matter with you this morning?' Tina had asked with a searching look.

'Nothing,' Cassie had said quickly. 'I'm just thinking about how much there is to do. I might as well go up to the Hall now, in fact. There's plenty to be getting on with. When Jake arrives, can you tell him I'm up there already?' she'd added casually, as if she wasn't counting the minutes until she saw him again.

She'd given herself a good talking-to as she walked up to the Hall. She'd hauled out all those well-worn arguments about being cool and professional, and concentrating on making the Hall a success, and had been so stern that she'd been feeling quite composed when she'd heard Jake's car crunching on the gravel outside.

So it had been unnerving to discover that all he had to do was walk in, looking lean and dark and forceful, for the air to evaporate from her lungs in a great whoosh. How could she think coolly and professionally when every cell in her body was jumping up and down in excitement at the mere sight of him?

Cassie swallowed and made herself shut up.

Jake was still inspecting the hall. 'It looks much better than it did,' he agreed. 'Are we still on target to have this room ready for the Allantide Ball? We're in October already,' he reminded her.

'It's only the fourth,' said Cassie. 'That gives us nearly a month until Hallowe'en. It'll be fine.'

It'll be fine. That was what she always said. Jake wasn't sure whether he envied Cassie her relaxed attitude or disapproved of it. There was so much about Cassie that made him feel unsure, he realised. Like the way he hadn't known whether he was looking forward to seeing her again or dreading it.

Jake didn't like feeling unsure, and that was how Cassie made him feel all the time. Ever since he had met her again, he seemed to have lost the control he had fought so hard to achieve.

Take that reception at the Savoy, when he had been so distracted by her that he had hardly been able to string two words together. Having to stand and watch Rupert kissing Cassie goodbye and slipping her his card had left Jake consumed by such fury that it was all he'd been able to do to stop himself from breaking Rupert's nose again. He'd had to remind himself that Cassie was probably delighted. She had told him herself of how she had dreamed of Rupert for years.

And, when it came down to it, she wasn't actually his fiancée, was she? Why was that so hard to remember?

Hating the feeling of things being out of his control, Jake had retreated into himself. He would focus on work. Work had got him where he was today, and it would see him through this odd, uncertain patch.

He had been glad when Cassie had said that she was going

down to Portrevick. It had felt like his chance to get some order back into his life—but the strange thing was that he had missed her. Her message about the photographs Tina's boyfriend had agreed to take had pitched him back into confusion again, but he hadn't been able to think of an excuse not to come, and then he had despised himself for needing an excuse. What was wrong with him? It was only Cassie.

Now he was here, and so glad to see her his throat felt tight and uncomfortable. At least she was dressed more practically today, in jeans and a soft red jumper, but he had forgotten what a bright, vibrant figure she was. It was like looking at the sun. Even when you dragged your eyes away, her image was burned onto your vision.

Jake cleared his throat. 'So, what's happening about these photos?'

'Oh, yes. Well, it's not a big deal. Rob is just going to take a few pictures of us inspecting the work here, maybe pretending to look as if we're making lists or looking at fabric samples. The idea is to have some "before and after" shots, but we don't need many now. We'll have to pull out the stops for the supposed "wedding" photos, but we'll do those after the Allantide Ball, when the great hall is finished and we can decorate it as if for Christmas.' Cassie looked at him a little nervously. 'Is that OK?'

'I suppose so,' said Jake. 'I can't say I'm looking forward to it, but we're committed now. We may as well get it over and done with.'

'Tina and Rob said they'd be here at five.' Cassie glanced at her watch. 'It's only three now. Do you want me to ring them and get them to come earlier?'

'What I'd really like is to stretch my legs,' said Jake. His gaze dropped to Cassie's feet. 'Those look like sensible shoes for once. Can you walk in them?'

Outside it was cool and blustery, and the sea was a sullen grey. It heaved itself at the rocks, smashing in a froth of white spray as they walked along the cliff tops. The coastal path was narrow, and the buffeting wind made conversation difficult, so they walked in silence—but it wasn't an uncomfortable one.

When at length they dropped down onto the long curve of beach, they were sheltered from the worst of the wind. Although Cassie's curls were still blown crazily around her head, it felt peaceful in comparison with the rugged cliffs.

'This was a good idea,' she said as they walked side by side along the tide line, their heads bent against the breeze and their hands thrust into their jacket pockets.

'It's good to get out of the car,' Jake agreed. 'Good to get out of London,' he added slowly, realising for the first time in years that it was true. He had been feeling restless and uneasy, but now, with the waves crashing relentlessly onto the shore, the wind in his hair and Cassie beside him, he had the strangest feeling of coming home. 'It's been…busy,' he finished, although the truth was that he had deliberately created work for himself so that he didn't have time to think.

'Has anyone said any more about our engagement?' Cassie asked after a moment.

'Nobody seems to talk about anything else,' said Jake. 'My staff are giving me grief that I haven't introduced you, and you've been specifically included in endless invitations to drinks and dinner and God knows what else. I'm running out of excuses.'

'I don't mind going,' said Cassie. 'But you probably don't want me to,' she added quickly. 'I know I don't exactly fit in.'

Jake stopped to stare at her. 'What do you mean?'

'I was so out of place at that reception,' she reminded him. 'I know I looked crass and ridiculous compared to everybody else there. It must have been really embarrassing for you.'

'I wasn't embarrassed,' he said. 'I was proud of you. You didn't look crass. You looked wonderful. Nobody could take their eyes off you. Do you have any idea of how refreshing you were?'

'Really?' she stammered, colouring with pleasure.

Jake began walking again. 'You ought to have more confidence in yourself,' he told her. 'You might not have a profession, but you've got social skills coming out your ears, and they're worth as much as any qualification. Look at what you've achieved down here.'

'I haven't really done anything,' said Cassie. 'The contractors are doing all the work.'

'They wouldn't be doing it if it wasn't for you. You had the idea; you're getting them all organised. It's time you stopped thinking of yourself as such a failure, Cassie.'

'Easy to say,' she said with a sigh. 'But it's hard when you've spent years being the under-achiever in the family. Social skills are all very well, but it's not that difficult to chat at a party.'

'It's difficult for me,' Jake pointed out. 'I never learnt how to talk easily to people. There were no parties when I was growing up, and precious little conversation at all. We didn't do birthdays or Christmas or celebrating.'

He walked with his eyes on the sand, remembering. 'My mother did her best, but there was never enough money, and she was constantly scrimping to put food on the table. She was a hard worker. She didn't just clean for Sir Ian, but at the pub and several other houses in the village. When she came home at night she was so tired she just wanted to sit in front of the television. I don't blame her,' he said. 'She had little enough pleasure in her life.'

And how much pleasure had there been for a little boy? Cassie wondered. Starved of attention, brought up in a joyless home without even Christmas to look forward to, it was no wonder he had grown up wild.

'It was hard for her trying to manage on her own,' Jake went on. 'I barely remember my father being at home. He was sent to prison when I was six. After he was released, he came home for a couple of weeks, but nobody in Portrevick was going to employ him. He went off to London to find a job, he said, and we never heard from him again.'

'I'm sorry,' said Cassie quietly, thinking of how far Jake had come since then. From village tearaway to chief executive in ten years was a spectacular achievement, and he had done it without any of the support she, her brothers and sister had taken for granted from their own parents. 'I can't imagine life without my dad,' she said. Her father might be a bit stuffy, but at least he was always there.

'You're lucky,' Jake agreed. 'I used to wish that I could have a father at home like everyone else, but maybe if he had been around I would have ended up following in his footsteps. As it was, I inherited his entrepreneurial spirit, but decided to stick to the right side of the law. But it was touch and go,' he added honestly. 'I was getting out of control. When you've got no money, no family life and no future, it feels like there's nothing to lose.

'Sir Ian's offer came just in time,' he said. 'It made me realise that I could have a future after all, and how close I'd come to throwing it away. I knew then that if I was going to escape I had to get myself under control. I built myself a rigid structure for my life. I worked and I focused and I got out of Portrevick and the mess my life had become, thanks to Sir Ian.'

He glanced at Cassie. 'But there wasn't much time along the way to learn about social niceties. You said you felt out of place at that reception, but you belonged much more than I did. I'm the real outsider in those situations. It's one of the reasons I was so drawn to Natasha,' he admitted. 'She fits in perfectly. I could go anywhere with her and be sure that she would know exactly what to do and what to say. It sounds pathetic, but I felt safe with her,' said Jake with a sheepish look.

'But you look so confident!' Cassie said, unable to put a lack of confidence together with her image of Jake, who had always been the coolest guy around. 'You were always leader of the pack.'

'In Portrevick, and the pack was a pretty disreputable one,' said Jake. 'And I can talk business with anyone. It's a different story in a smart social setting, like that reception, where you're supposed to know exactly how to address Lord This and Lady That, how to hold your knife and fork properly, and chit-chat about nothing I know anything about.

'You could do it,' he told Cassie. 'You chatted away without a problem, but I can't do that. It makes me feel…inadequate,' he confessed. 'It's one of the reasons I resent Rupert so much, I suppose. He's colossally arrogant and not particularly bright, but he can sail into a social situation and charm the pants off everyone. Look at what he was like with you,' said Jake bitterly. 'All over you like a rash, and never mind that you're supposed to be my fiancée and I'm standing right there.'

'I think it's just an automatic reflex with Rupert,' said Cassie, hugging this hint of jealousy to her. 'He flirts with every woman he meets.'

'Does he give them all his number and tell them to call him?'

'Probably,' she said. 'And most of them no doubt will ring him. But I'm not going to. I've thrown his card away.'

Jake felt a tightness in his chest loosen. 'Good,' he said, and when he looked sideways at Cassie their eyes snagged as if on barbed wire. Without being aware of it, their steps faltered and they stopped.

Cassie was intensely aware of the dull boom of the waves crashing into the shallows, of the familiar tang of salt on the air, and the screech of a lone gull circling above. The wind blew her hair around her face and she held it back with one hand as she finally managed to tear her eyes from Jake's.

He looked different down here on the beach, more relaxed, as if the rigid control that gripped him in London had loosened. She was glad that he had told her more about his past. It sounded as if his childhood had been much bleaker than she had realised, and she understood a little better now why he had been so insistent on a formula for relationships. If you had no experience of an open, loving relationship like her parents', fixing on a partner who shared your practical approach must seem a much better bet than putting your trust in turbulent emotions that couldn't be pinned down or analysed.

It was sad, though. In spite of herself, Cassie sighed.

Beside her, Jake was watching the wet-suited figures bobbing out in the swell. Even at this time of year there were surfers here. Portrevick was a popular surfing beach, and lifeguards kept a careful eye from a vehicle parked between the two flags that marked the safe area.

Following his gaze, Cassie saw one of the surfers paddling furiously to pick up a big wave just before it crested. He rose agilely on his board, riding the wave as it powered inland, until the curling foam overtook him and broke over him, sending him tumbling gracefully into the water.

'Why don't you surf any more?' she asked him abruptly.

'I can't.'

'But you were so good at it,' Cassie protested. 'You were always in the water. I used to watch you from up there,' she said, pointing up to the dunes. 'You were easily the best.'

Jake's mouth twisted. 'I loved it,' he said. 'It was the only time I felt really free. When things got too bad at home, I'd come down here. When you're out there, just you and the sea, you feel like you can do anything. There's nothing like the exhilaration you get from riding a big wave, being part of the sea and its power...' He trailed off, remembering.

'Then why not do it again?'

'Because...' Jake started and then stopped, wondering how to explain. 'Because surfing is part of who I was when I was here. I don't want to be that boy any more. When I left Portrevick, I cut off all associations with what I'd been. I wanted to change.'

'Is that why you gave up riding a motorbike too?'

He nodded. 'Maybe it's not very rational, but there's part of me that thinks the surfing, the bike, the risks I used to take, all of those were bound up with being reckless, being wild and out of control. It felt as if the freedom they gave me was the price I had to pay to get out of Portrevick and start again.'

'But you've changed,' said Cassie. 'Taking out a surf board or riding a motorbike isn't going to change you back.'

'What if it does?' countered Jake, who had obviously been through this many times before. 'What if I remember how good it felt out there? I'm afraid that, if I let go even for a moment, I might slide back and lose everything I've worked so hard for. I can't risk that. My whole life has been about leaving Portrevick behind.'

He was never going back, Jake vowed. No matter if here, by the sea, was the only place he ever felt truly at home. He had escaped, and the only way was forward.

'It seems a shame,' said Cassie. 'You can't wipe out the past. That wild boy is still part of who you are now.'

'That's what I'm afraid of,' said Jake.

Who was she to talk, anyway? Cassie asked herself as they turned and walked slowly back along beach. She didn't want to be the gauche adolescent she had been, either. Perhaps if she could put her past behind her as firmly as Jake had she too could be driven and successful, instead of muddling along, living down her family's expectations.

Tina and Rob were waiting for them back at the Hall, and Rob took a series of photos. 'Detailed shots are best,' Tina said authoritatively. 'I've been looking through a few bridal magazines, and that's what the readers want to see. A close up of a table decoration, or your shoes or something, so they can think, "ooh, I'd like something like that".'

'What about a close up of the engagement ring, in that case?' Jake suggested.

'That's a brilliant idea. Why aren't you wearing it, Cassie?'

'It feels all wrong to wear it all the time,' said Cassie, taking the box out of her bag and slipping the ring onto her finger. 'It's not as if it's a real engagement ring.' Unaware of her wistful expression, she turned her hand to make the jewels flash. 'It's just a prop.'

'Some prop,' said Tina, admiring it. 'It's absolutely gorgeous—and perfect for you, Cassie.'

'It's beautiful, isn't it?' Cassie's eyes were still on the ring. 'Jake chose it.'

Tina's sharp gaze flicked from her friend's face to Jake, who was watching Cassie. 'Did he now?'

Cassie was glad they had had that talk on the beach. Things were much easier between them after that, and they were able to chat quite comfortably when Jake gave her a lift back to London the next day.

She understood a little more why he was so determined to leave his old life behind him, and could admire the way he had transformed himself—but a little part of Cassie was sad too. Their conversation had underlined yet again how very different they were. She wished Jake could let go just a little bit, just enough to let him want someone a little muddled, a little messy.

A little bit like her, in fact.

Oh yes, and how likely is that? Cassie asked herself. Jake was used to a woman like Natasha, who was beautiful and clever and fit perfectly into his new life. Why on earth would he want to 'let go' for *her*? The best she could hope for was to be a friend.

And that was what she would be, Cassie decided. After the photo session, she had persuaded Jake to come to the pub with her, Tina and Rob. He had been reluctant at first, remembering the less-than-warm welcome he had had on previous occasions, but this time it was different. Cassie had made sure that Portrevick knew the truth about Sir Ian's will, and word had got round about the Allantide Ball too. She was determined to see Jake accepted back in the village, whether he liked it or not.

So the drive back to London was fine. Or, sort of fine. It

was comfortable in one way, and deeply uncomfortable in another. A friend would enjoy Jake's company, and that was what she did. A friend would ask him about his time in the States and about his job, and chat away about nothing really. A friend would make him laugh.

But a true friend *wouldn't* spend her whole time having to drag her eyes away from his mouth. She wouldn't have to clutch her hands together to stop them straying over to his thigh. She wouldn't drift off into a lovely fantasy, where Jake would pull off the road and rip out her seatbelt in a frenzy, unable to keep his hands off her a moment longer.

'Quick—where's the nearest Travelodge?' he would say—except a motel was a bit tacky, wasn't it? Cassie rewound the fantasy a short way and tried a new script. 'Let's get off the main road and find a charming pub with a Michelin-starred restaurant and a four-poster bed upstairs,' she tried instead.

Yes, that was more like it, she decided, almost purring in anticipation. There would be a roaring fire and they would sit thigh-to-thigh in front of it with a bottle of wine…then Jake would take her hand and lead her up some rickety stairs to their bedroom. He'd close the door and smile as he drew her down onto the bed, unbuttoning her blouse and kissing his way down her throat at the same time.

'I've been thinking about this for weeks,' he would murmur, his lips hot against her skin, his hands sliding wickedly over her. 'I'm crazy about you.'

'I love you too,' she would sigh.

'Did you mean what you said?' said Jake, startling her out of her fantasy at just the wrong point.

'What?' Cassie jerked upright, her blood pounding. Good grief, she hadn't been dreaming aloud, had she? 'No! I mean…when? What did I say?'

'On the beach yesterday. You said you wouldn't mind coming along to various events as my fiancée again?'

Cassie fanned herself with relief. 'Oh…no, of course not.'

Willing her booming pulse to subside, she pulled at her collar in an attempt to cool herself. She had got a bit carried away there. *I love you too*. What on earth was that about? She wasn't in love with Jake. What a ridiculous idea. She just… found him very attractive.

Yes, that was all it was.

On the other hand, friendly was all she was supposed to be, she reminded herself sternly. 'I'm always up for a party.'

Keep it light, Cassie had told herself. But it didn't stop her spending hours searching for the definitive little black dress when Jake rang and asked if she could come to a drinks party later that week.

She should have spared herself the effort. Jake hated it. 'It's boring,' he said when Cassie presented herself with a twirl and made the mistake of asking what he thought. 'Why didn't you buy a red one? Or a green one? Anything but black!'

Cassie was crestfallen. 'I thought you'd like it if I wore what everyone else was wearing,' she said. 'I didn't want to stand out.'

'I like you as you are,' said Jake.

When Cassie thought about it afterwards, she realised that it was actually quite a nice thing for him to say, but the words were delivered in such a grumpy, un-lover-like tone that at the time she was rather miffed. She had thought she looked really smart for once.

She didn't bother dressing up for the day at the spa. To Jake's horror, *Wedding Belles* had decided to send a photographer along to take a picture of them enjoying their prize, so Cassie had to hurriedly arrange a day when they could make the most of the voucher. Jake was furious when he heard that he had to take a day off work.

'It'll be good for you,' Cassie told him. 'You need to relax. I'll book some treatments.'

'There had better not be any seaweed involved,' warned

Jake as they signed in to the spa, which promised them 'utter serenity'... 'a time out of time'.

'Don't worry,' said Cassie. 'I knew you didn't like the idea of seaweed, so you're going to be smeared in mud from the Dead Sea, and then wrapped in cling film instead.'

'What?'

She rolled her eyes and laughed at his aghast expression. 'Oh, don't panic. You're just getting a back massage. It'll help you unwind.'

Jake was deeply uncomfortable about the thought of a massage at all, but in the end it wasn't too bad. He couldn't say he found the spa a relaxing experience, though. There was nothing relaxing about spending an entire day with Cassie, dressed only in a swimming costume and a fluffy robe which she cast off frequently as she dragged him between steam rooms, saunas and an admittedly fabulous pool.

How could he relax when Cassie was just *there*, almost naked? Jake couldn't take his eyes off her body. She wasn't as slender or as perfectly formed as Natasha, but she had long, strong legs and she was enticingly curved. She looked so *touchable*, thought Jake, his mouth dry.

He had to keep dragging his eyes back to her face as she sat on the edge of the pool, dangling her legs in the water, or stretched out on the pine slats in the sauna, chatting unconcernedly. The photographer took a snap of them in their robes, and Jake had a feeling that he was going to look cross-eyed with the effort of keeping his hands off that lush, glowing body.

Utter serenity? Utter something else entirely, in Jake's book!

He told himself that it would be a relief when Cassie went back to Portrevick to prepare for the Allantide Ball. But as soon as she had gone he missed her. It was almost as if he was getting used to her colourful, chaotic presence; as if a day without seeing her walk towards him on a pair of ridiculously unsuitable shoes, or hearing her laugh on the end of the phone, was somehow dull and monochrome. Cassie enthused by email from Portrevick:

Wait till you see the great hall! It's looking fab. As soon as ball is over, will redecorate as if for a Christmas wedding and Rob is all teed up to come and take some photos of us. Will send them to *Wedding Belles* in January, and then it'll all be over, you'll be glad to know! Cxxx

Jake spent a long time looking at those three kisses. Kiss, kiss, kiss. What kind of kisses did she mean? Brief, meaningless, peck-on-the-cheek kisses? Or the kind of kisses that made your heart thunder and your head reel? The kind of kisses you couldn't bear to stop, but were never enough? She had added,

P.S., We're having an evening wedding (just so you know!) so don't forget your tuxedo!

But all Jake saw was 'it'll all be over'. He wasn't sure that he wanted it to be over, and not being sure threw him into turmoil. For ten years now he *had* been sure. He had known exactly what he needed to do. Now Cassie had thrown all that into question with three little kisses.

CHAPTER NINE

'WHAT do you think?' Cassie gestured around the great hall, and Jake turned slowly, staring at the transformation she had wrought.

From the ceiling hung a mass of paper lanterns, gold, red, russet and orange, their autumn colours investing the great hall with a vivid warmth. Everywhere else in the country rooms were being decorated with pumpkins, ghoulies and ghosties for Hallowe'en, but here in Portrevick Hall there were candles in every stone niche and great bowls piled high with Allan apples, just as there had been in Sir Ian's time.

Outside, it was cold and damp. Fallen leaves were lying in great drifts and the air held an unmistakable edge, with the promise of winter blowing in from the sea, but inside the Hall was warm and inviting.

'It looks wonderful,' said Jake sincerely. He couldn't believe how Cassie had transformed the Hall in such a short time. He couldn't quite put his finger on what she had done. It was as if she had waved a wand and brought the old house to life again. 'You've done an amazing job,' he told her.

Cassie coloured with pleasure. 'I'm glad you like it. I think it'll look good in the photos. The local paper are sending someone to cover the ball, and they're going to mention the fact that the Hall is being developed as a venue—so that should get us some coverage locally, at least.

'Oh, by the way,' she said, carefully casual, 'word has got out about our supposed engagement, so I thought I'd better move into the Hall with you. It's not as if we're short of bedrooms here, and it might look a bit odd if I was engaged to you but still staying chastely with Tina.'

'Fine,' said Jake, too heartily. The idea of Cassie moving in with him was like a shot of adrenalin. He knew quite well that she wouldn't be sharing a bedroom with him, but still there was a moment when the blood roared in his ears and he felt quite lightheaded. 'Good idea.'

He cleared his throat, wondering how to get off the subject of bedrooms. 'How many people are you expecting tonight?' he asked Cassie.

'I'm not sure. Probably about a hundred and fifty or so,' she guessed. 'More or less the same as usual. Everyone I've spoken to in the village has said they're coming.'

She didn't add that she suspected that most of them were curious to see Jake again. 'I've put notices up in the local pubs, the way Sir Ian used to do, so we may have some people from round about, too.'

Jake ran his finger around his collar. 'I'm not sure how I feel about confronting so much of my past in one fell swoop,' he admitted.

'It'll be fine.' Cassie laid a hand on his arm, her brown eyes warm. 'Everyone knows the truth about Sir Ian's will. They're prepared to accept you for how you are now.'

Jake didn't believe that for a moment, but he was too proud to admit that he was dreading the evening ahead. 'What time are they all coming?'

'Seven o'clock.' Cassie looked at the old clock still ticking steadily after all these years. 'We'd better get changed.'

'I hope you're not wearing that black dress again,' said Jake as they moved towards the stairs.

'No,' she said. 'You made such a fuss about that, I thought I'd wear a red one this time.'

'A red one?' Jake paused with one foot on the first step. 'Like the one you wore to the last Allantide Ball?'

Their eyes met, and the memory of how they had kissed that evening shimmered in the air so vividly that Cassie could almost reach out and touch it. A tinge of colour crept into her cheeks. 'I hope this one is a little more classy.'

'Shame,' said Jake lightly. 'Does that mean you're not going to flirt with me again?'

'I might do,' said Cassie, equally lightly, but the moment the words were out she wanted to call them back. If she was going to flirt with Jake, was she going to kiss him too? The question seemed to reverberate in the sudden silence: *did flirting mean kissing…kissing…kissing?*

She swallowed and set off up the stairs. 'Only if I have time—and nothing better to do, of course.' She tried to joke her way out of it.

'Of course,' Jake agreed dryly.

'Use this bathroom here,' he said, leading her down a long, draughty corridor. He pointed at a door. 'It's the warmest, and the only one with halfway decent plumbing.'

Cassie tried to calm her galloping pulse as she showered and changed into the dress she had bought after Jake had so summarily rejected her foray into black elegance. This one was a lovely cherry-red, and the slinky fabric draped beautifully over her curves and fell to her ankles. It had a halter neck and a daringly low back. Her mother would have taken one look at it and told her that she would catch her death and should cover up with a cardigan, but Cassie wasn't cold at all. The thought of Jake in the shower just down the hall was keeping her nicely heated, thank you.

She leant towards the mirror to put on her make-up, but her hand wasn't quite steady; she kept remembering the look in Jake's eyes when he'd asked if she was going to flirt with him the way she had ten years ago.

She was no good at this 'just being friends' thing, Cassie

decided. A friend would have treated his question as a joke. Had she done that? No, she had given him a smouldering look under her lashes. *I might do*, she had said.

Cassie cringed at the memory. Good grief, why hadn't she just offered herself on a plate while she was at it? She would have to try harder to be cool, she decided. But she couldn't stop the treacherous excitement flickering along her veins and simmering under her skin as she slid the ruby ring onto her finger, took a deep breath and went to find Jake.

He was still in his room, but the door was open. Cassie knocked lightly. 'Ready?' she asked.

'Nearly.' Jake was fastening his cuffs, a black bow-tie hanging loose around his neck. Glancing up from his wrists, he did a double take as he saw her standing in the doorway, vibrant and glowing in the stunning red dress.

For a moment, he couldn't say anything. 'You look…incredible,' he said, feeling like a stuttering schoolboy.

'Thank you.'

Mouth dry, Jake turned away. 'I'll be with you in a second,' he managed, marvelling at how normal he sounded. 'I just have to do something about this damned tie.' He stood in front of the mirror and lifted his chin, grimacing in frustration as he attempted to tie it with fingers that felt thick and unwieldy. 'I hate these things,' he scowled.

'Here, let me do it.' Cassie stopped hovering in the doorway to come and push his hands away from the mess he was making with the tie. 'I deal with these all the time at weddings. Stand still.'

Jake stood rigidly, staring stolidly ahead. He was excruciatingly aware of her standing so close to him. He could smell her warm, clean skin, and the fresh scent of her shampoo drifted enticingly from her soft curls, as if beckoning him to bury his face in them.

In spite of himself, his gaze flickered down. Cassie's expression was intent, a faint pucker between her brows as she concentrated on the tie with deft fingers. He could see her dark lashes, the sweet curve of her cheek, and he had to clench his fists to stop himself reaching for her.

'OK, that'll do.' Cassie gave the tie a final pat and stood back. And made the fatal mistake of looking into his eyes.

The dark-blue depths seemed to suck her in, making the floor unsteady beneath her feet, and her mind reeled. Cassie could feel herself swaying back towards him, pulled as if by an invisible magnet, and her hands were actually lifting to reach for him when Jake stepped abruptly back.

'Thank you,' he said hoarsely, and cleared his throat. 'That looks very professional.'

Cassie's pulse was booming in her ears. She moistened her lips. 'I should go down—see if the caterers need a hand.'

She practically ran down the stairs. Oh God, one more second there and she would have flung herself at him! It had taken all her concentration to fasten that tie when every instinct had been shrieking at her to rip it off him, to undo his buttons, to pull the shirt out of his trousers and press her lips to his bare chest. To run her hands feverishly over him, to reach for his belt, to drag him down onto the floor there and then. What if Jake had seen it in her eyes?

Well, what if he had? Cassie slowed as she reached the bottom of the staircase. It wasn't as if either of them had any commitments. They were both single, both unattached. Why *not* act on the attraction that had jarred the air between them just now?

Because Jake had felt it too, Cassie was sure.

The prospect set a warm thrill quivering deep inside her. It grew steadily, spilling heat through her as she helped a tense Jake greet the first arrivals, until she felt as if she were burning with it.

Cassie was convinced everyone must be able to see the naked desire in her face, but if they could nobody commented. There was much oohing and aahing about the decorations instead, and undisguised curiosity about Jake and their apparent engagement, of course. But nobody seemed to think that there was anything odd about the feverish heat that must surely be radiating out of every pore.

She kept an anxious eye on Jake, knowing how much he had been dreading the evening. He might not think he could do social chit-chat, but it seemed to Cassie that he was managing fine. Only a muscle jumping in his cheek betrayed his tension. She had felt him taut beside her at the beginning, but as he relaxed gradually Cassie left him to it. Standing next to him was too tempting, and it wouldn't do to jump him right in front of everyone.

Smiling and chatting easily, she moved around the Hall. Having grown up in Portrevick, she knew almost everyone there, and they all wanted to know about her parents, brothers and sister. Normally, Cassie would have been very conscious of how unimpressive her own achievements were compared to the rest of the family's, but tonight she was too aware of Jake to care. She talked about how Liz juggled her family and her career, about Jack's promotion, about the award Tom had won—but her attention was on Jake, who was looking guarded, but obviously making an effort for the village that had rejected him.

Cassie was talking to one of her mother's old bridge friends when she became aware of a stir by the main door, and she looked over to see Rupert and Natasha stroll in, looking impossibly glamorous. Her first reaction was one of fury—that they should turn up, tonight of all nights, to make the ball even more difficult for Jake than it needed to be.

Jake had his back to the door and hadn't seen them yet. Cassie excused herself and hurried over to intercept Rupert and Natasha. 'I'm surprised to see you here,' she said, although she was more surprised at how irritated she was by Rupert's ostentatiously warm greeting.

'I saw the ball advertised, and thought we would drop in for old times' sake,' said Rupert. 'After all, Sir Ian *was* my uncle.' He looked nostalgically around the great hall. 'Besides, I wanted Natasha to see the house where I grew up.'

'You only came for part of the summer holidays,' Cassie pointed out, knowing that what Rupert really wanted to do was flaunt Natasha in front of Jake and remind him of his humiliation.

'Now, why do I get the impression you're not pleased to see me, Cassie?' Rupert smiled and leant closer. 'Or is it possible that you're not pleased to see Natasha?' he murmured in her ear.

Natasha, looking cool and lovely, was standing a little apart, her green eyes wandering around the great hall. She might have been admiring the architecture, but Cassie was sure that she was searching for Jake, and her lips tightened.

'Oh, dear, I suppose it was a bit tactless of us to come,' Rupert went on with mock regret. 'Jake did adore her so, and you can see why. She's perfection, isn't she?'

'She's very beautiful,' Cassie said shortly, thinking that that really was tactless of Rupert. As Jake's fiancée, she was hardly likely to want to hear about how much he had loved another woman, was she? 'But looks aren't everything, Rupert. Jake's in love with me now.'

'Is he?' Rupert's smile broadened as he looked down into Cassie's face. 'You don't think there could be a little touch of the rebound going on? Or even, dare I say it, a little face-saving, hmm? He did get together with you very quickly after Natasha left, after all.'

Cassie met his amused blue eyes as steadily as she could. Rupert might be extraordinarily handsome, but he wasn't stupid. 'Think what you want, Rupert,' she said as she turned on her heel. 'Jake loves me and I love him.'

She heard the words fall from her lips, and the truth hit her like a splash of cold water in her face: she *did* love Jake. Why hadn't she realised it before? It had snuck up on her without her realising.

Trembling as if she had had a shock, Cassie looked around for Jake and caught a glimpse of him through the crowd, standing almost exactly where he had been standing ten years ago. He was momentarily alone, looking dark and formidable, and the sight of him was like a great vise squeezing her entrails.

Cassie knew why she hadn't wanted to see the truth. It was impossible that a man like Jake could love her back. Rupert was right, of course. Jake had adored Natasha. He had told her so himself, hadn't he? If he had indeed felt the...*something* fizzing between them, Cassie was fairly sure that he would think of it as no more than a physical attraction.

Well, that might be enough, Cassie told herself as she wove her way through the chattering groups towards him, very aware of Rupert's mocking gaze following her. She would convince him that what was between her and Jake was real—even if it wasn't—and, if that meant seducing Jake, so much the better.

She wouldn't fool herself that it could last for ever, but she could at least make the most of the time she did have with him. She could save Jake's face and assuage the terrible need that was thudding and thumping in the pit of her belly at the same time.

So she smiled at Jake and ran her hand lightly down the sleeve of his dinner jacket, hoping if nothing else to distract him from the fact that Natasha and Rupert were here. 'I thought I'd come and see if my flirting technique is any better than ten years ago.'

Amusement bracketed his mouth, but his eyes were hot and dark as they ran over her. 'The thing about wearing a dress like that is that you don't need to flirt. You don't need to say anything at all. You just need to stand there and look like that.'

Cassie swallowed. 'Gosh, you're much better at flirting than I am!'

'You haven't even started yet,' Jake pointed out. 'I'm waiting for you to do your worst. Get those eyelashes batting!'

The dark-blue gaze came up to meet hers, and their smiles faded in unison. 'Come on—flirt with me, Cassie,' he said softly, and her breath snared in her throat.

Her heart, which had been pounding away like mad, had decelerated suddenly to a painful slam, so slow that she was afraid that it might stop altogether.

'I...can't,' she whispered, unable to tear her eyes from his, and Jake lifted a gentle hand to run a finger down her cheek, searing her skin with its caress.

'Shall we skip the flirting, then?' His voice was very deep and very low. 'Shall we just go straight to the kissing?'

Unable to speak, Cassie nodded dumbly. She had forgotten Rupert, forgotten Natasha, forgotten that they were surrounded by the whole of Portrevick. As far as she was concerned, they could sink right down onto the stone flags together and make love right there. But Jake, more aware of everyone around them, took her hand and pulled her out along the corridor and onto the side terrace, just as he had done ten years ago.

Like then, it was cold and drizzly, but neither of them noticed. The door banged behind them, and Jake was already sliding his fingers into Cassie's hair the way he had fantasised about doing for so long. His mouth came down hungrily on hers and they kissed fiercely, almost desperately.

Cassie grabbed his shirt, holding on to it for dear life; suppressed excitement was unleashed by the touch of his lips and rocketed through her so powerfully that she could have sworn she felt her feet leave the ground.

God, it felt so good to be kissing him! He tasted wonderful, he felt wonderful, so hard, so strong, so gloriously, solidly male. She slid her arms around him to pull him tighter, her pulse roaring in her ears, as Jake backed her into the wall, his hands moving possessively, insistently, over her, making her dress ruck and slither, smoothing warm hands down her bare back.

'I've wanted this for weeks,' he whispered unevenly in her ear, when they broke for breath.

'I think I've wanted it for ten years,' she said, equally shaky.

'Liar,' Jake laughed softly, but his mouth was drifting down her throat, making her gasp and arch her head to one side. 'You wanted Rupert.'

It was hard to think clearly with his lips teasing their way along her jaw and his fingers tracing wicked patterns on her skin. 'I don't want Rupert now,' she managed raggedly, clutching her hands in his dark hair. 'I want *you*.'

Jake lifted his head at that and took her face between his hands, looking deep into her eyes. 'Are you sure, Cassie?'

'Oh yes,' she said, reaching for him again. 'I'm quite sure.'

Cassie drew a long, shuddering sigh of sheer pleasure and snuggled closer into Jake. Her head was on his shoulder, and his arm was around her, warm and strong, holding her securely as they waited for their heart rates to subside and their breathing to steady. She suspected Jake had fallen asleep, but her blood was still fizzing with a strange mixture of peace and exhilaration. She could feel herself glowing, radiating, shimmering with such contentment that she was surprised she wasn't lighting the dark room. Plug her in and she could power a chandelier, if not a city full of street lights. They could keep her as an emergency back-up for the energy crisis. Who needed a nuclear power-station when all Jake had to do was make love to her like that?

Somehow they had got themselves from the terrace to Jake's room. Cassie had no idea whether anyone had seen them and she didn't care. Nothing had mattered but Jake: the feel of him, the taste of him, the sureness of his hands, the delicious drift of his lips, the hard possession of his body.

Cassie felt giddy just thinking about that heady blur of sensation. They had lost all sense of time, of place. Nothing had existed except touch—*there...there...yes, there...yes, yes*—need so powerful that it hurt, and excitement that spun like a dervish, faster and faster, terrifyingly faster, until they lost control of it and it shattered in a burst of heart-stopping glory.

Downstairs, Cassie could hear the muted sounds of the Allantide Ball still in full swing without them, and felt sanity creeping back. It wasn't entirely welcome, she realised, and wondered if Rupert was still down there.

And Natasha.

What was it Rupert had said? *A little touch of the rebound going on? Jake did adore her so.*

He had. Cassie remembered him telling her about Natasha the first time they had driven down here together. *She's perfect,* he had said. She was everything he'd ever wanted.

Which made her just someone to catch him on the rebound.

Cassie sighed and stroked the broad chest she was resting so comfortably against. What did she have to offer, after all? Look at her, the failure of her family. She wasn't beautiful, wasn't successful, wasn't accomplished, wasn't calm and sensible. She couldn't begin to compare with Natasha.

On the other hand, she was here, lying next to Jake, and Natasha wasn't.

She would have to keep her fantasies firmly under control for once, Cassie vowed. There was no point in getting carried away like she usually did. She wasn't Jake's dream, and she never would be. Best to face it now.

But she didn't have to think about the future yet. She had the here and now. Cassie rested her palm over Jake's heart and felt it beating steadily. For now that was enough.

'We'd better get on.' Cassie sighed and stretched reluctantly. November had dawned dark and dank, and she would have loved to stay snuggled up to Jake's warm, solid body all day. 'There's lots to do.'

Lazily, Jake slid his hand from the curve of her hip to her breast, and she caught her breath at the heart-stopping intimacy of the gesture. 'Like what?' he asked, pulling her closer.

'Like getting married,' she reminded him, and laughed as

he froze for a moment. 'I can't believe you've forgotten that Tina and Rob are coming tonight for another photo session!'

'I've had other things on my mind,' said Jake, rolling her beneath him, lips hot and wicked against her breast, making her arch beneath his hands. 'More important things—like reminding you what you've been waiting ten years for…'

Here and now, Cassie told herself as desire flooded her. Jake was right. What was more important than that?

It was much later when she finally forced herself out of bed, and nearly had a fit when she saw the time. 'There's so much to do!'

Fortunately the caterers had cleared up most of the debris from the party the night before, but they still had to take down the Allantide decorations and make the great hall look as if it was Christmas instead.

'Why don't we leave it until it *is* Christmas?' asked Jake as Cassie ran around putting up fairy lights and piling pine cones into bowls.

'Because I was trying to get everything over as soon as possible,' she said. 'I thought it made sense to do all the photos at once. Rob said he took some good ones last night, which we can use on the website, and I've arranged for him to come back tonight since you'd be down here anyway. I didn't think you'd want to come down more than you had to.'

'I don't mind,' said Jake, who couldn't quite remember now why he had been so resistant to the idea. He couldn't remember much about anything this morning except how warm, sweet and exciting Cassie had been the night before.

He felt as if he were walking along the edge of a cliff, knowing that a false step would send him tumbling out of control. Jake wasn't sure how he had got himself there, but he couldn't turn round and go back now. He had to keep going and not look down to see how far it was to fall.

They hadn't talked about the future at all, and Jake was glad. He had a feeling that even thinking about a future that accommodated Cassie, and the chaos she took with her wherever she went, would send his careful life slipping over the edge of that cliff.

The sensible thing, of course, would have been to remember that before he had made love to her. But he was here now, and Cassie's bright presence was lighting up the great hall. He could be sensible again when he got back to London.

'If we left it until December, you could have a Christmas tree,' he pointed out.

Cassie hesitated, picturing a tall tree in the corner by the staircase. 'It would look lovely,' she admitted. 'But everything else is ready now. I've got my dress on loan, as it's just going to be used for photographs, and Rob and Tina are all sorted too. We might as well go ahead,' she decided reluctantly. A Christmas tree would have been the perfect finishing touch.

She was setting a round table as if for a reception, and Jake was astounded by the detail. She seemed to have thought of everything, from carefully designed place-card holders to tiny Christmas puddings on each plate. A stunning dried-flower arrangement with oranges and berries in the centre of the table held candles, wine glasses were filled with white rose-petals, and silver crackers added a festive touch.

'How on earth did you think of all this?' he asked. He would have thrown on a tablecloth, and might have risen to a candle or two, but that was where his inspiration would have run out.

'Oh, it was easy,' said Cassie, straightening the last cracker and standing back to survey the table with satisfaction. 'This is my job, remember? Besides, all I had to do in this case was act out a fantasy I've had for years,' she went on cheerfully. 'I always wanted a Christmas wedding, and in my fantasy it was here at the Hall, so I didn't really have to think of anything. I knew exactly what I wanted.'

Of course, in her fantasy Rupert would probably have been the groom, Jake thought jealously.

Cassie was chattering on. 'Naturally, there would be lots

more tables if this was a real wedding. I'm hoping Rob will be able to take some pictures of us that will give the impression that hundreds of guests are milling around in the background. We'll feel complete prats, I know, but it's all in a good cause, and if Rob can get some good shots of details the Hall should look wonderful in that article.'

Ah yes, the article. Jake had almost forgotten why they were doing this.

'It does look surprisingly Christmassy,' he said, looking around. He wasn't sure how Cassie had done it. There were no snowmen or reindeer, no Santa Claus climbing down the chimney. Instead she had created a subtle effect with colour and light.

'Wait till we've lit the fire and the candles,' said Cassie. 'I've made some mince pies too, and some mulled wine to offer our guests as they come in from the cold. Rob can take a still-life shot and then we might as well enjoy them to get us in the mood.'

'All you need is some mistletoe,' said Jake.

'It's too early, unfortunately, but don't think I haven't tried to get some!'

'Let's pretend it's hanging right here,' he said, pointing above their heads and drawing Cassie to him with his other arm. 'Then I can kiss you right underneath it.'

Dizzy with delight, Cassie melted in to him and wound her arms around his neck to kiss him back.

'When are Tina and Rob coming?' Jake's voice was thick as he nuzzled her throat, making her shiver with anticipation.

Cassie opened her mouth, but before she could say anything the old-fashioned door-bell jangled.

Jake sighed. 'Now?'

'I'm afraid so.'

Tina gasped at the transformation Cassie had wrought on the great hall. 'It feels like Christmas already! I can feel a carol coming on… O come, all ye faithful,' she warbled tunelessly.

They left Rob taking photos of the table and decorations while they went to change. Tina had bought a black-evening dress, which they had decided would be suitable for a brides-maid, and she helped Cassie into the borrowed wedding-dress. Made of satin and organza, it was fitted underneath with a floaty outer layer that was fixed at the waist with a diamond detail.

'Oh Cassie, you look beautiful,' Tina said tearfully as she fastened a simple tiara into Cassie's hair. The curls didn't lend themselves to a sophisticated up-do, and in the end Cassie had decided to leave her hair as it was and save on the expense of a hairdresser.

'Hey, I'm not really getting married,' she reminded Tina, but her expression was wistful as she studied her reflection. It was her dream dress, and it was impossible not to wish that she was wearing it for real.

Jake waited in the great hall with Rob as she and Tina headed down the grand staircase. Without the bother of make-up, it hadn't taken him long to change into his tuxedo again. He stood at the bottom of the stairs watching Cassie coming down, and looking so devastating. Her knees felt weak and her mind spun with the longing to throw herself into his arms.

And then she almost did as she missed a step and lurched to one side. She would have fallen if Tina hadn't grabbed her and hauled her upright. 'God, you're such a klutz, Cassie,' her friend scolded. 'It won't make much of a photo with you lying at the bottom of the stairs with a broken neck!'

Then Cassie was all fingers and thumbs as she attempted to pin a white-rose buttonhole on Jake. 'I'll do it,' he said in the end, and she turned away to pick up the bouquet she had ordered, only to fumble that too. Jake caught it just before it hit the ground, and shook his head. 'You're hopeless,' he said, but he was smiling.

Get a grip, Cassie, she told herself sternly.

'So, what's the idea?' said Tina, getting down to business. 'Are you having the wedding here too?'

'No, just the reception,' said Cassie who had managed to pull herself together. 'We've been married in Portrevick church, and we've just arrived in a horse and carriage.'

Jake made a face. 'A car would be much more sensible. It's a steep hill up from the village.'

'Yes, well, this is a fantasy,' said Cassie a little crossly. 'Who wants a sensible fantasy? It was a horse and carriage,' she insisted. 'A *white* horse, in fact. Or possibly two.'

'OK,' said Rob, breaking into the discussion. 'I've taken as many details as I can. Let's have the bride and groom looking into each other's eyes.'

He posed them by some candles Cassie had lit, and while he fiddled with his camera Cassie adjusted Jake's bow tie. 'You look very nice,' she said approvingly.

'And you look beautiful,' said Jake.

A jolt had shot through him as he had looked up to see her coming down the staircase, and he was feeling jarred, as if it was still reverberating through him. The dress was white and elegantly floaty. She looked glamorous and sexy and, yes, beautiful.

And then she had stumbled, and he hadn't been able to resist smiling, pleased to see that it was Cassie after all and not some elegant stranger.

Unable to resist touching her, he ran his hands up her bare arms. 'It's Christmas Eve. Weren't you a bit chilly in that carriage?' he said, trying to lighten the atmosphere, trying to loosen whatever it was that had taken such a tight grip on his heart when he had looked up to see Cassie as a bride.

'I had a *faux* fur stole to wear when we came out of the church,' she explained.

'And a muff, I hope?' said Jake, remembering Michelle at the wedding fair, and they both started to laugh at the same time.

They had forgotten Tina and Rob, who was snapping away. They had forgotten the article, forgotten why they were dressed up as a bride and groom. They had forgotten everything except the warmth and the laughter—then somehow they weren't laughing any more, but were staring hungrily at each other.

'That's great,' called Rob from behind his camera. 'Now, what about a…?'

He tailed off, realising that Cassie and Jake weren't even listening.

'A kiss,' he finished, but they were already there. Cassie was locked in Jake's arms, and they were kissing in a way that would have raised a few eyebrows at a real wedding, where kisses for the camera were usually sweet and chaste. There was nothing sweet or chaste about this kiss.

Rob looked at Tina, who rolled her eyes. 'Guys? *Guys!*' she shouted, startling Jake and Cassie apart at last. 'You're embarrassing Rob,' she said with a grin as they looked at her with identically disorientated expressions. 'These photos are supposed to be for a brides' magazine, not something they keep on the top shelf! They don't want pictures of the wedding night, just a sweet little peck on the lips so the readers can all go "aah".'

'Sorry, yes, I suppose we got a bit carried away,' said Cassie, flustered.

'A bit? We didn't know where to look, did we, Rob?'

'It must have been all the time shut up in that carriage,' muttered Jake, alarmed at how easily he lost control the moment he laid hands on Cassie.

They posed for a whole ream of photographs, but at last Rob decided that he had enough. 'I'll send you the link so that you can look at them online,' he told Cassie. 'And then you can pick a selection of the best to send to *Wedding Belles* after Christmas.'

Jake couldn't wait for Rob and Tina to be gone. He closed the door after them with relief and turned back to Cassie, who was blowing out the candles.

'Now, where was that mistletoe again?' he said, and she

beckoned him over so that she could put her arms around his neck and kiss him.

'Right here,' she said.

CHAPTER TEN

'I've got to go back to London this afternoon,' said Jake the next morning as they lay in bed. Realising how reluctant he was to go sent him teetering perilously on the edge of that sheer drop again, though, and he shied away from the thought. He smoothed the curls back from Cassie's face. 'Do you want a lift?'

Keep it light, he told himself. Offering a lift back to London wasn't the same as suggesting that she move in with him, have his baby or anything that smacked remotely of commitment. It was just saving a train fare.

'I can't,' sighed Cassie. 'I promised to meet one of the contractors tomorrow to talk about electrics. Now that the hall is done, we need to start work on the kitchens and bathrooms. There's still a long way to go before we can open as a venue. I really need to stay another couple of days.'

Jake was horrified by how disappointed he was at the prospect of three nights without her, but perhaps a few days apart wasn't a bad thing. It would give him a chance to get himself under control and start thinking clearly again. He wasn't himself when Cassie was right there, warm, soft and desperately distracting. It was too easy to lose control, too easy to forget what he risked by letting go of his careful, ordered life.

So when Cassie said that she would be back in London on Wednesday he made himself hold back. He didn't offer to meet her at the station, take her out to dinner or take her back to his apartment to see how she looked amongst his furniture, the way he really wanted to do. 'Give me a ring when you're back,' was all he said.

Right. Not 'I'll miss you'. Not 'I love you'. Not even 'I'll call you', thought Cassie. But what had she expected? Jake was a careful man nowadays. He might have made love to her with a heart-stopping tenderness and passion, but he wasn't about to rush into a relationship with her.

And quite right too, Cassie reminded herself. She had decided that the here and now was enough for her, and it was obviously enough for Jake as well. So she smiled as she kissed him goodbye after lunch and waved him off to London.

She ought to be happy, she thought as she went back inside and began the dreary task of taking down the Christmas decorations. She had had the most wonderful weekend. OK, so Jake hadn't said that he wanted to see her again, but he hadn't said that he *didn't* want to, either. He couldn't have made love to her like that if he didn't feel anything, could he?

They had all the photos they needed for the article, so there was no real need for him to come down to Portrevick again. But he might need her to be his fiancée again in London. It would look suspicious if they broke off their supposed engagement just yet. They had agreed that they would keep the pretence going until after Christmas, and that was still weeks away, Cassie reassured herself. It was only the beginning of November. Anything could happen in that time.

Just because Jake hadn't talked about the future didn't mean they couldn't have one.

Still, Cassie couldn't help feeling bereft now that he had gone. She wandered disconsolately around the great hall, taking down the fairy lights and dismantling the table she had laid so carefully the day before.

When the bell jangled, she hurried to open the massive

front door, relieved at the distraction. She hoped it would be
Tina, who had promised to come and give her a lift back to
the village. A good chat with her old friend was just what she
needed. But when she threw the door open wide, the smile was
wiped from her face. It wasn't Tina who stood there.

It was Natasha.

'Oh!'

Natasha smiled a little hesitantly. 'Hi,' she said.

'I'm afraid Jake isn't here,' said Cassie, unable to think of
any other reason Natasha would be here on her own. 'He's
gone back to London.'

'Actually, it was you I was hoping to see. Have you got a
moment?'

The last person Cassie wanted to talk to right then was
Natasha, but she couldn't think of a polite way to refuse.
'Sure,' she said reluctantly, and stood back. 'Come in.'

Gracefully, Natasha stepped into the hall. Swathed in a
fabulous cream cashmere pashmina, she stood looking beautiful and making everything around her seem faintly shabby
in comparison.

Including Cassie.

There was an awkward silence. 'Would you like some
tea?' Cassie found herself asking to her own disgust.

'That would be nice, thank you.'

'We'll go to the kitchen. It's warmer there.'

Cursing her mother's training, which meant that you
always had to be polite whatever the cost, Cassie led the way
to the kitchen.

Natasha sat at the table, unwinding her pashmina to reveal
an exquisite pale-blue jumper, also cashmere by the look of
it, and Cassie sighed as she filled the kettle. If she tried to wear
a top that colour, she would spill something down it and ruin
it two seconds after she had put it on, but Natasha looked as
if she had stepped out of the pages of a magazine.

Switching on the kettle, she turned and leant back against

the worktop and folded her arms. 'What did you want to talk to me about?'

'About Jake,' said Natasha.

Cassie stiffened. 'What about him?'

'I just wanted to know…how he is.' Natasha moistened her lips. 'I'd hoped to see him at the ball the other night, but I couldn't find him.'

Cassie thought about what Jake had been doing while Natasha had been looking for him, and her toes curled. 'He's fine,' she said shortly.

'I see,' whispered Natasha, and to Cassie's horror the green eyes filled with tears. 'I'd hoped…I'd hoped…'

'That he'd be pining for you?'

'Yes.' She nodded miserably. 'I've been such a fool,' she burst out. 'Rupert—he was like a madness. I've always been so sensible, and to be pursued like that by someone so glamorous and so exciting, well, I was flattered. You know what Rupert's like.'

'Yes, I know,' said Cassie. 'But I know what Jake is like too, and so should you. He's worth a thousand Ruperts, and he deserved better than being left without warning—and for Rupert of all people! You must have known how humiliating that would be for him,' she said accusingly.

Natasha bit her lip. 'I can see that now, of course I can, but at the time I wasn't thinking clearly.'

Dropping her head into her hands, she clutched her perfectly straight blonde hair with her perfectly manicured fingers. 'It sounds crazy now, but I just lost my head. I was tired of being clever and careful and doing the right thing all the time. Rupert was such fun and so seductive. Being with him seemed like my only chance to do something wild and spontaneous. It was like my own little rebellion.'

'A little self-indulgent, don't you think?' said Cassie, unmoved. 'Couldn't you have found a way to have fun and be *spontaneous* that didn't involve hurting Jake?'

'I never meant to hurt him, you must believe that!' Natasha lifted her head to look at Cassie with imploring green eyes. 'We never had a very demonstrative relationship. I suppose other people would have looked at us and thought we were cool, but I didn't appreciate what I had. I thought I wanted something different, but then I didn't like it. The truth is that I'm not a rebel. I'm conventional. I'm careful. I like a plan, just like Jake. With Rupert, I never know where we're going to be or what we'll be doing, and I hate it!

'I miss Jake,' she said on a sob, and the tears spilled over at last. 'When I'm with him, I feel so safe. We had so much in common. We were perfect together, but I treated him so badly, and now I don't know if he'll ever forgive me.'

Cassie poured boiling water onto two tea bags. Her face felt tight. Her heart felt tight. 'Why have you come to me?' she asked coolly, squeezing the bags with a spoon before fishing them out.

Natasha wiped tears from under her eyes. Predictably, she was one of those women who looked beautiful even when they were crying. When Cassie cried, she went all blotchy, her nose ran and her eyes turned piggy.

'Because Rupert said he doesn't think you're really engaged to Jake,' said Natasha in a rush. 'He thinks Jake is just saving face, and if…if that's true…then I would like to go to him, to tell him how desperately sorry I am that I hurt him, and ask if he'll give me another chance. I swear I would never do anything like this again,' she promised, an edge of desperation in her voice. 'I can be what Jake needs, I know I can.'

Tight-lipped, Cassie handed Natasha a mug and pushed the carton of milk towards her. She wasn't ready to prove Rupert right just yet, and besides there was last night. Everything had changed now.

Hadn't it?

'And what *does* Jake need?' she prevaricated.

'He needs someone who'll make him feel safe too,' said Natasha. 'I know what a struggle it has been for him to get where he is now. He needs someone who'll let him forget the past and love him for the person he is now. Someone who understands what drives him and doesn't try to challenge him.'

No, thought Cassie instinctively. She shook her head. 'I think you're wrong,' she said. 'Jake shouldn't forget the past. He needs to accept it, accept that it's part of him. You can't just pretend the past never existed.'

'If someone doesn't want to talk about their childhood, you should respect that,' said Natasha. 'Jake knew I would never press him about it. It's one of the reasons he felt comfortable with me.'

Cassie could feel herself prickling with irritation. 'Jake deserves more than comfortable, Natasha,' she said. 'He needs laughter and love and passion and—and *acceptance* of who he was and who he is.'

'I can give him all of that,' said Natasha defensively. 'I do accept him. If I didn't, I would want to change him, and I don't. He doesn't need to change for me.'

But perhaps he needed to change for himself.

Jake needed to let down his guard, to throw away his rule book and his specifications and let himself love and be loved—but that would mean him giving up control, and Cassie wasn't sure he would be able to do that.

He didn't believe in love. Jake had made that very clear. He thought all you needed for a successful relationship was a formula, and Natasha fitted his specifications perfectly. He had told her that.

They had agreed that they were completely incompatible. Two nights weren't going to change that, were they?

Cassie's heart cracked. She so wanted to believe that this magical weekend had been the start of something wonderful, but what, really, did she have to go on? When Jake kissed her, when his hands drifted lazily, possessively, over her body, she hadn't needed to hear that he loved her. Then, the here and now had been enough, but now he had gone, and she could feel her confidence leaking out of her in the face of Natasha's glowing beauty.

It was too easy now to wonder if he had turned to her on the rebound from Natasha, if he had simply been looking for someone different to distract him from the hurt and the humiliation of being left by the woman he really wanted.

Now, too late, she could remember that it had only ever been a pretence, and Jake had never suggested otherwise. Why hadn't she remembered that before?

Because it wasn't a pretence for her, not any more. Cassie loved Jake. She knew that she could give him what he really needed.

But what he needed wasn't necessarily what he wanted.

Stirring her tea, Cassie looked across the table at Natasha, who had dried her tears and was looking poised and elegant once more.

Looking exactly like the kind of woman Jake had aspired to for so long.

A lead weight was gathering in Cassie's chest as she remembered everything Jake had ever told her. He didn't want to take the risk of falling in love. He didn't want to lose control. He didn't want to change.

Natasha could give him so many of things he had said he *did* want. She wouldn't push him. She would let him keep his emotions all buttoned up—and wasn't that, really, all Jake wanted?

Strange that she and Natasha should love the same man when they were so different, Cassie thought. There was Natasha: so beautiful, so sensible, so classy and so cool, representing the future Jake had worked so hard for—and there was her; clumsy, messy Cassie who muddled through and did her best but would never be more than an also-ran. Who would always be associated with the past he resented so much.

Did she really think Jake would rather be with her than Natasha?

Better to face reality now, Cassie decided. She wasted too much of her life dreaming as it was. This time, she would be the sensible one.

Natasha had been watching her face. 'Is it true?' she asked quietly. 'Is Jake just trying to save face by pretending to be engaged to you?'

Cassie looked down at the ruby ring which she had never got round to taking off the night before. Very slowly, she drew it off and dropped it onto the table, where it clattered and rolled for a moment before toppling over.

'Yes,' she said. 'It's true.'

'You did *what*?' said Tina in disbelief. She had arrived about ten minutes after Natasha had left to find Cassie a sodden mess in the kitchen.

'I told Natasha the truth.'

'And sent her back to Jake with *your* ring? You're mad, Cassie! You and Jake had something really good going there.'

'We were just pretending,' said Cassie drearily, blowing her nose. Unlike Natasha, she wasn't a pretty sight when she cried, and she had just cried more than she had ever cried before.

Tina wasn't having any of it. 'Don't give me that. I saw the way you kissed each other last night. There was nothing fake about that. Good grief, the top of my head practically blew off, and that was just watching you!' She put her hands on her hips and shook her head at Cassie. 'I can't believe you'd just give up and let that drippy Natasha swan back to him. It's not like you to be so wet. You're crazy about Jake, and you just gave him up without a fight. What's that about?'

'Because it's not a fight I could ever win,' Cassie said miserably. Did Tina think she hadn't thought about it? 'We're completely incompatible.'

'You looked pretty compatible to me last night.'

Cassie's eyes filled with tears again and she swiped angrily at them with the back of her hand. 'We want different things, Tina. Jake thinks he can order a relationship like everything else, and I'm holding out for something he thinks doesn't exist. I want someone to love me, someone who needs me as much as I need him. Jake thinks that's a fairy tale.'

'I'm sure he does love you, Cassie,' said Tina, putting an arm around her shoulders. 'He may not realise it yet, that's all. I bet you anything he'll send Natasha away with a flea in her ear, and come roaring back down here with that ring as soon as he hears what you've done.'

But Jake didn't come. On Wednesday, Cassie sent him a brief, businesslike email saying that she was staying in Portrevick for a while to oversee work on the Hall. She didn't mention Natasha, and nor did Jake when he replied.

Thanks for update, was all he said. *Keep me posted. Regards, Jake.*

Regards? *Regards?* Was that all he could say after he had rolled her beneath him and smiled against her throat? After his hands had unlocked her, made her gasp and arch? After he had loved her slowly, thoroughly, gloriously, and held her, still shaking, as they spiralled back to reality together?

How dared he? Furious, Cassie stabbed at the delete button. How dared he send her *regards* after he had made her love him?

Sheer anger kept her going all afternoon, but when it leaked away it left her more miserable than ever.

'Tell him how you feel,' said Tina, exasperated. 'Put yourself in Jake's shoes. He's got no idea that you care for him at all. You have a great weekend together, and the next thing he knows you've tossed him back his ring and told Natasha he's all hers. What's the poor bloke supposed to think?'

'What am *I* supposed to think?' Cassie protested tearfully. 'He didn't even suggest meeting up in London.'

'He's probably terrified you'll think he's getting too heavy.

If you ask me, you're both being big babies,' said Tina. 'At least Natasha had the guts to go and tell him how she felt.'

The mention of Natasha was enough to plunge Cassie back into the depths. 'How can I go? He'll be back with Natasha by now.' She tortured herself by imagining the two of them together. How could Jake have resisted those green eyes shimmering with love and the promise of calm? When Cassie looked at herself in the mirror she saw eyes puffy with tears, awful skin and limp hair. There was no way Jake would want her now, even if he wasn't dazzled anew by Natasha's beauty.

At least work on the Hall was going well, she tried to console herself. Joss was pleased with the way the project was going, and as November was never a busy time for weddings she was happy for Cassie to stay in Cornwall for the time being. It was bittersweet, being up at the Hall every day, but Cassie threw herself into the job. It was all she had left.

Three long, wretched weeks dragged past. The days got shorter, darker and damper, and Cassie got more miserable. It was time to go back to London and pick up her old life, she decided grimly. She had been perfectly happy before, and she would be again. It wasn't as if she was likely to bump into Jake. London was a big city and their lives would never cross, unless he was tactless enough to ask her to plan his wedding to Natasha. Cassie couldn't see that happening. No, she would go back, stick to the job she could do and stop trying to be someone she wasn't.

'I'll be back tomorrow,' she told Joss, and went for a last walk on the beach. The sea was wild, the sky as grey as her mood. It was very cold, and the spray from the crashing waves stung her cheeks.

Head bent, Cassie trudged along the sand. There were no surfers today, no lifeguards, and she had the beach to herself. Except, she realised, for a figure in black leathers that was heading towards her from the dunes. Some biker who must have left his motorbike in the car park, and, not content with roaring through the villages disturbing everyone's peace, was now spoiling her solitude.

Cassie scowled. There were plenty of other empty beaches in Cornwall at this time of year. Why did he have to come here? She wanted to be miserable on her own, thank you very much.

And he was coming straight for her! Cassie glared at him, and was just about to turn pointedly on her heel when she stopped. Hang on, wasn't there something familiar about that walk? About that self-contained stride? She looked harder. The set of those shoulders, the darkness of the hair…. It couldn't be, could it?

All at once a great hand seemed to close tight around her, inside her, gripping her heart, her lungs and her entrails so that she couldn't breathe. She could just stand and stare, brown eyes huge with disbelief and desperate hope, as he came closer and closer until he was standing right in front of her.

'So this is where you are,' said Jake.

'Jake.' It came out as little more than a squeak.

Cassie was completely thrown, ricocheting around between astonishment, sheer joy and confusion at how different he looked. Standing there in black leather, he seemed younger, wilder, and the guarded look she had become used to had been replaced by a reckless glint. The wind ruffled his hair, and with the angry sea behind him he looked so like the old Jake that she could hardly speak.

'What…what are you doing here?' she stammered at last.

'Looking for you,' said Jake.

He sounded the same. He just looked so… Cassie couldn't think of a word to describe how he looked, but it was making her heart boom so loudly that it drowned out the crashing waves and the wind that was whistling past her ears.

She swallowed hard. This, remember, was still the Jake who had gone back to London without a word about the future, who had sent her his *regards*.

'What for?' she asked almost rudely.

'I bought a motorbike,' he said. 'I wanted to show you. Everyone thinks I'm having a midlife crisis, but I thought you would understand.'

'I would?'

'You were the one who said that riding a bike wouldn't change me, that I could let go just a little and I wouldn't lose everything I'd fought to be.'

Cassie eyed the leathers. They made him look lean, hard and very tough. Of course, he looked like that in a suit too, but now he was even more unsettling. 'I'm not sure I was right about that,' she said. 'You look like you've changed to me.'

'But I haven't,' said Jake. 'I'm still Chief Executive of Primordia. I still have my MBA, my experience, my career. My world hasn't fallen apart because I bought a bike. I really thought that it would,' he said. 'I was afraid that I might lose myself, but I've found myself instead. I've realised that I can't change the past. I have to accept that my family, my past, that difficult boy I was, all of them are part of who I am now.' A smile lurked in his eyes as he looked at Cassie. 'You were right about that too.'

Cassie moistened her lips. 'I don't think I've been right so often before,' she tried to joke, not knowing what else to do, not knowing what was happening, knowing only that all her certainties were being shaken around like flakes in a snow globe.

'You weren't right about Natasha,' said Jake. 'You sent her to me because you thought she was what I wanted, didn't you?'

'She is what you want.' It was cold in the wind, and Cassie hugged her jacket about her. By unspoken consent, they turned their backs to the wind and started walking back along the beach, the sand damp and firm beneath their feet.

Cassie dug her hands in her pockets and hunched her shoulders defensively. 'You told me she was,' she reminded him. 'You told me she was perfect.'

'I thought she was,' he admitted. 'I thought I needed

someone cool and careful, like I was trying so hard to be. I thought I needed someone who would help me fit in, who would help me forget what I'd been and where I'd come from.'

'Someone like Natasha,' said Cassie bitterly.

'Yes. I thought Natasha was exactly what I needed, but I was wrong,' said Jake. 'It took meeting you again to realise that what I really needed was someone who would make me laugh, who would give me the strength to let go of everything I thought I needed.' He slowed, and Cassie slowed with him, until they had stopped and were facing each other alone on the beach.

'Someone who would make me remember, not forget,' he said, his voice very deep and low. 'Someone who would force me to stop running away from the life I had here and accept it as part of who I am.'

He looked down at Cassie, whose hands were still thrust into the pockets of her jacket, and he could see the realisation of what he had come to say dawning in the brown eyes.

'Someone like you,' he said.

'But—but, Jake, you can't need me,' she said in disbelief, even as Jake was reaching for her wrists and tugging her hands gently from her pockets. 'I'm the last person you can want. I'm not sensible or clever or beautiful or—or *anything*,' she said, but her fingers were twining of their own accord around Jake's. 'I'm useless.'

'Useless?' he said. 'You've transformed the Hall, organised a ball, set up a wonderful marketing opportunity with a magazine, charmed the socks off everyone who met you in London. You're not useless at all,' he said sternly.

'My family wouldn't agree with you,' she sighed. 'I haven't achieved anything, not like the rest of you, with your degrees and your fantastically successful careers.'

'But you can do the things your clever, successful family can't.'

'Oh yes? Like what?'

'Like make the sun seem brighter when you smile,' said

Jake. 'Like making me laugh. Like making me happy.' He drew her closer. 'Like making me safe,' he said softly. 'Cassie, tell me I can do that for you too.'

Her eyes filled with tears. 'You can,' she whispered. 'You do.'

They didn't kiss, not at first. They just held each other, very, very tightly. Cassie's face was pressed into his throat, and she could smell the leather of his jacket, just as she had done ten years ago. But this time the shock and anger had gone and in their place was a ballooning sense of joy and relief, as if she had finally found her way home.

Safe—that was what Jake had said he felt. Cassie knew exactly what he meant.

'Tell me you love me, Cassie,' he murmured against her hair, and she tipped back her head to smile at him, her eyes still shimmering with tears.

'I love you,' she said. And then they did kiss, a long, intoxicatingly sweet kiss that dissolved the hurt and the uncertainty and left them heady and breathless with happiness.

'I love you,' said Jake shakily at last. Somehow they had made it to the shelter of the dunes, and sank down onto the soft sand as they kissed and kissed again. 'I love you, I love you,' he said again between kisses. 'I can't tell you how much.'

Cassie drew a shivery sigh of sheer contentment and rested her head on his shoulder, her arms wound tightly around him as if she would never let him go. 'What about the formula?'

'Ah, the formula,' he said with a wry smile. 'I clung to that formula like a life raft! It seemed to make sense,' he tried to explain. 'It worked, or at least it did until I met you again. You don't know what you did to me, Cassie. You turned my world upside down. I had constructed such a careful life, and suddenly everything was out of control.

'You made me *feel* again, and I was torn. I wanted you, but I didn't want you. You were part of the past I'd been running away from for so long. I thought if I could just hold onto my sensible, practical formula I'd be all right, but I can see now that it was just as much a fantasy as the fairy tale that you believe in.'

'Yes, I've learnt that too,' said Cassie, snuggling closer as they lay in the sand. 'I held on to the fairy tale, just like you held on to the formula. I suppose I was always such a dreamer that it was natural for me to fantasise about the perfect relationship, the perfect wedding, the perfect everything.'

She ran her hand over his abdomen. Even through the leather, she could feel the muscled strength of him. 'I don't think you're perfect, though.'

'Oh?' Jake pretended to sound hurt, and she softened the blow by leaning up on her elbow and smiling down at him as she dropped a kiss on his lips.

'No, you're not perfect. You're impatient and practical and oh-so-sensible—or you were until you went out and bought yourself a motorbike just to make a point! When I dreamed of the man I would love, I never imagined someone like you, but it *is* you. I've learnt to love what's in front of me, not a dream. Now I know that you love me back, well…' She smiled, kissing him again. 'I think this just might be the fairy tale after all!'

She settled back into the curve of his arm with a sigh of happiness. 'I've been so wretched for the last three weeks,' she told him. 'Why did it take you so long to come?'

'Because I thought you'd changed your mind after I'd gone,' said Jake. 'I thought you'd just been amusing yourself that weekend, and that you didn't want to get any more involved. I thought you couldn't even be bothered to tell me yourself. You just sent Natasha instead.'

Cassie wriggled uncomfortably. 'I didn't *send* her. I thought you would be happy to see her.'

'Happy? Hah!' Jake snorted. 'There was one moment that day when I was wildly happy. The door bell rang and I convinced myself that it was you, that you'd told the contractors they could go to hell so that you could come up to London early and be with me.'

'Well, I don't know why you would think I would do that.' Cassie pretended to grumble. 'You never said a word. How was I to know you wanted to see me?'

'I know, I was a fool. I should have begged you to come with me.' Jake wound his fingers in the curls that were hopelessly tangled by wind and sand. 'But, Cassie, I was terrified,' he said. 'I'd fallen wildly in love with you. That weekend, when we made love, it all happened so fast. I felt as if I was losing control when I was with you, nothing else mattered. I could feel myself slipping back, becoming the reckless boy I'd been before, not caring about anything except the moment.

'It was as if everything I'd spent the last ten years working for had started to crumble,' he tried to explain. 'I thought I needed a day or two to get a grip of myself and decide what I really wanted.

'And I realised that I wanted *you*,' he told her. 'When I got to London, everything was colourless without you. That life I'd fought to keep under control was still under control, but it was flat and meaningless too. So I knew I wanted you, but I wasn't sure how to win you. You were always telling me how incompatible we were, and you clearly didn't need *me* to have a good time.'

Jake paused. 'There was a little bit of me, too, that was hung over from the past, a bit that didn't feel as if I was good enough for you. You come from such a nice, happy, middle-class family, and when all was said and done I was still one of those Trevelyans with a father in prison.'

'But you're more than that,' said Cassie. 'Your family doesn't matter. It's you I love, and as for my family, well, they're going to see a chief executive, not the wild boy who used to make trouble in the village. They like high achievers, remember? They'll approve of you much more than they do of me!'

'I hope so,' said Jake. 'I suppose I just lost my nerve in London. I told myself I had to take things carefully, so I planned to ask you out to dinner as soon as you got back and ask if you'd consider making that silly pretence of being engaged real. But Natasha turned up instead. She told me you'd admitted that it was just a pretence, and had sent back the ring to prove it.'

'I didn't think you'd be able to resist her,' sighed Cassie. 'She's so beautiful.'

'Well, yes, she is—but next to you she's just a little colourless. I never laughed with her the way I laughed with you. We never talked, or argued, or lost our cool with each other. Natasha's a nice person,' said Jake. 'But she was the last person I wanted to see that day. Once I'd got over my disappointment that she wasn't you, we had a long talk. I think the fact that she was ready to have an affair with Rupert made her realise that we weren't really right for each other. I hope she'll find the right man one day, but it's not me.'

'Why didn't you at least call me *then*?' asked Cassie, thinking of the weeks they had wasted being miserable apart.

'I was angry,' said Jake. 'With Natasha, with you, but mostly with myself—for letting myself fall in love with you, for throwing my whole life into disorder for someone who apparently didn't care enough about me to tell me she couldn't be bothered to carry on pretending. And then, when I *did* hear from you, it was just an impersonal email about the Hall!'

'At least I didn't sign it "regards"!' sniffed Cassie, and he laughed as he hugged her closer.

'I was trying to show you I cared as little as you did. God, I can laugh now, but at the time I was hurt and I was bitter. I was impossible to deal with for two weeks—my PA told me she was ready to shoot me, in the end—until I realised I couldn't go on like that. I used to take myself off for long walks around the streets, and one day I passed a guy on a motorbike. It was just like the one I used to have in Portrevick, and that's when I started to think about what you'd said about accepting the past and letting go of it at the same time.

'I can take a risk, I thought, and I went out and bought a

bike of my own. And then I took an even bigger risk. I thought you'd be back in London, so I went round to your office and Joss told me you were still here, so I got straight on my bike and drove all the way down here,' he said, unzipping a pocket to pull out the ruby ring.

He shifted so that he was lying over Cassie, smiling down into her eyes. 'I came to tell you that I love you and I need you, and that more than anything in the world I want you to take this ring back and say you'll marry me. Will you, Cassie?'

Cassie's smile trembled as she took the ring and slid it back onto her finger where it belonged. 'Oh yes,' she breathed, and her eyes shone as she put her arms around Jake's neck to tug him down for a long, long kiss. 'Oh yes, I will.'

The short winter afternoon was closing in, but it was only the first spots of rain that forced them to move at last. 'Have you still got that wedding dress you wore for the photos?' Jake asked as they brushed sand off each other.

'I took it back to the shop the next day.'

'Why don't you go and buy it?' he said. 'We can get married at Christmas.'

'Christmas!' said Cassie, startled. 'That's only a month away!'

'It's enough time for the banns to be read.'

'Just!'

'And the wedding's already planned,' he pointed out as they headed back to the car park. 'We've got the table decorations and we know the menu. We've even had the photos done already. Tina's got her bridesmaid's dress, and I've got my tuxedo—unless you want me in breeches and a cravat, of course! So all you need to do is buy the dress and tell your family.'

'Are you sure you don't mean next Christmas?' asked Cassie. 'What happened to Mr Sensible? I thought you'd be saying it was crazy to rush into marriage!'

'It is,' said Jake with a smile. 'But let's do it anyway.'

A gleaming, mean-looking motorbike had the car park to

itself. Jake handed Cassie a helmet when they got back to it and put on his own. 'Hop on the back,' he said, kicking the machine into gear. 'And we'll go and see if the vicar can fit us in for a Christmas wedding.'

EPILOGUE

Christmas Eve

CASSIE woke on her wedding morning to a glittering world. Under a thin, blue winter sky, a hard frost rimed every twig and every blade of grass. But by lunchtime the clouds had blanked out the meagre December light, hanging so heavily they seemed to be muffling the slightest noise, and Portrevick was enveloped in the stillness and strange, expectant silence that comes before snow.

In the pub, they were taking bets on a white Christmas at last, and the children were wild with excitement at the prospect of bulging stockings and presents under the tree. Cassie had always loved Christmas, too, but this was her wedding day, and all she was dreaming about was the moment she stood in front of the altar with Jake. Until then, she hardly dared let herself believe that it wasn't just all a dream.

At four o'clock it was already dark, but there were flares lining the path to the church, and the trees were strung with fairy lights. Tina took the *faux* fur stole Cassie had worn on the brief journey from Portrevick Hall with her father and laid it on the porch seat.

Cassie's father offered her his arm. 'You look beautiful, darling,' he said. 'Your mother and I are very proud of you,

you know.' His voice cracked a little at the end, and he had to clear his throat.

'Thank you, Dad.' Cassie's eyes stung with tears. 'Thank you for everything.'

'Promise me you'll be happy with Jake.'

'I will.' It was her turn to swallow a huge lump in her throat. 'I know I will.'

'In that case,' said her father, reverting to his more usual, reassuringly brisk manner. 'Let's go.'

And then they were walking up the uneven aisle of the old church. *How odd*, Cassie found herself thinking with a strange, detached part of her mind. She had spent so long planning weddings for other brides, so many years dreaming about her own, that she thought she would know how it would feel.

Everything looked exactly as she had always imagined it. Lit only by candles, the little church looked beautiful, and was filled with the people she loved. Her mother was there, trying not to cry. Liz had started already, and was wiping her eyes with a handkerchief as she smiled tremulously. Her brothers were doing their level best to look as if they weren't moved, and not quite succeeding.

The flowers were simple, stunning arrangements of white, and tiny wreaths hung at the end of every pew. Cassie had a blurred impression of warmth and colour as everyone turned to smile as they passed. Yes, it was just as she'd imagined it.

What she had never imagined was that none of it would really matter. The only thing that mattered was that Jake should be there, waiting for her at the altar.

And there he was. Cassie's heart gave a great bound of relief as she saw him turn. He was looking serious, but as she got closer she saw that he was not serious so much as anxious, and she knew with a sudden, dazzling certainty that he had been afraid she wouldn't come, that all that mattered to him was that *she* was there.

Her father lifted her hand to his lips and kissed it, and

Cassie smiled at him brilliantly before he stepped back to join her mother. Then she turned to face Jake at last.

He smiled at her as he took her hand, and she smiled back, twisting her fingers around his. All at once it was just the two of them in the warm candlelight. They had forgotten the church and the watching congregation, and Cassie could feel herself beginning to sway towards him, turning her face up for his kiss already.

The vicar cleared his throat loudly, and they turned to him with identically startled expressions. He smiled. 'If you could spare us few minutes of your attention...?' he murmured.

'Sorry,' they whispered back, and he raised his voice.

'Dearly beloved...'

The familiar words rang like a bell in Cassie's heart. This was what her wedding was about. It wasn't about the beautiful dress she was wearing, or the gasps when the guests saw the great hall. It was more than an excuse for a party. It was about Jake and about her, about the love they shared and the life they would build together.

Her eyes never left Jake's dark-blue ones. She was intensely aware of his hand, of his voice making his responses steadily, of the smooth coolness of the ring he slid onto her finger. At last she was in the right place at the right time. It wasn't a dream. This was where she was meant to be, and this was the man she was meant to be with.

Cassie's heart was so full, she could hardly say 'I do'. Even when she thought it couldn't possibly be any fuller, it kept swelling, and swelling until the vicar declared them man and wife, and then she was afraid it would explode altogether. Giddy with happiness, she smiled as Jake took her face between his hands and kissed her.

'You look beautiful,' he said.

Cassie had seen how radiant other brides looked, and now she knew exactly how they felt. She was brimming with joy. It felt as if it were spilling out of her, shimmering away into the candlelight.

In a blur, she dropped the pen twice before she managed to sign the register, and then she was sailing back down the aisle, Jake's fingers wrapped firmly round her own.

The church doors were thrown open and a magical scene awaited them. Great, soft snowflakes were drifting steadily to the ground, blurring the warm, flickering glow of the flares and glimmer of the tiny lights in the trees.

'Oh Jake, it's perfect!' gasped Cassie, and promptly tripped over the porch step. 'Just as well we decided not to have a video,' she muttered out of the corner of her mouth as Jake hauled her upright, and behind her she heard Tina smother a fit of giggles. 'Thank goodness I had you to hang on to, or I'd have gone flat on my face!'

Jake's hand tightened and he smiled down at her. 'That's the thing about being married,' he said. 'We'll always have each other to hang on to now.'

Cassie's smile widened. 'So we will,' she said, and then stopped, catching sight of a carriage drawn up outside the lych gate. In the light of the flares there, she could see that it was pulled by two white horses.

A car would be more sensible, Jake had said once, and it was a car she had expected to take them back to the great hall. But Jake, her sensible husband, must have remembered her fantasy and arranged the carriage for her instead.

Her eyes shone as she looked up at him. 'It's my dream!' she breathed, but Jake shook his head and smiled.

'It's not a dream,' he said. 'It's real.'

* * * * *

This season we bring you
Christmas Treats

*For an early Christmas present,
Jessica Hart would like to share
a little treat with you...*

JESSICA HART'S TOP TEN TIPS
FOR A SPARKLING CHRISTMAS PARTY!

1. Invite all your neighbours as well as your friends, even if you don't know them very well. Everybody loves to be invited to a party—and it's a great way to meet that person you smile at in the street every day but whose name you don't know...

2. It's much more fun if everyone is jammed in together, so put your guests in a room that's not quite big enough for them all. Don't let anyone sit down, either! It makes it easier for your guests to mingle and meet each other if everyone is standing up.

3. Don't forget to introduce guests to each other—it can be daunting to walk into a room full of people who all seem to know each other, and it makes a big difference if the hostess makes sure everyone has someone to talk to when they arrive.

4. At Christmas you can go to town on the decorations—a Christmas tree is a must, but fairy lights look wonderful strung around the room too. Keep the lighting flattering with candles and soft lamps, and put out piles of pine cones and crackers. A room fragrance scented with cinnamon, oranges and cloves will get everyone in the mood the moment they step through the door.

5. Greet guests with a glass of mulled wine and a mince pie as soon as they arrive, or impress them with a real Christmas cocktail—see below!

6. Cheese biscuits to nibble on are easy to make, and if you buy a box of Christmas pastry-cutters you can have holly,

stars, angels, Christmas trees and all sorts of other Christmassy shapes, or use letters to spell Noel or Happy Christmas on a plate. They can be made in advance, and will make it look as if you've gone to masses of effort even when you haven't.

7. Have a Secret Santa. Give all your guests a (very low) price limit and get everyone to bring a present to put beneath the tree. That way everyone will have a gift to take home—but much more fun will be had watching their reactions as they open their present!

8. Make sure you leave yourself enough time to make yourself look fantastic. It won't matter if nothing else is ready as long as you're there to greet people when they arrive.

9. Don't forget the music—the cheesier, the better. Bring out all the old Christmas favourites and your guests will dance the night away.

10. Have a good time and everyone else will too!

JESSICA HART'S CHRISTMAS COCKTAIL

Frost the glasses in advance by dipping the rims first in lightly whipped egg white, and then in caster sugar.

Put a sugar cube in the bottom of each glass and add enough brandy to cover. Let it soak for a while, then pour in some cranberry juice and top with sparkling wine.

Stand back and watch your party take off!

*Celebrate 60 years of pure reading pleasure
with Harlequin®!
Just in time for the holidays,
Silhouette Special Edition® is proud to present
New York Times bestselling author
Kathleen Eagle's
ONE COWBOY, ONE CHRISTMAS*

Rodeo rider Zach Beaudry was a travelin' man—until he
broke down in middle-of-nowhere South Dakota during
a deep freeze. That's when an angel came to his rescue....

"Don't die on me. Come on, Zel. You know how much I love you, girl. You're all I've got. Don't do this to me here. Not *now*."

But Zelda had quit on him, and Zach Beaudry had no one to blame but himself. He'd taken his sweet time hitting the road, and then miscalculated a shortcut. For all he knew he was a hundred miles from gas. But even if they were sitting next to a pump, the ten dollars he had in his pocket wouldn't get him out of South Dakota, which was not where he wanted to be right now. Not even his beloved pickup truck, Zelda, could get him much of anywhere on fumes. He was sitting out in the cold in the middle of nowhere. And getting colder.

He shifted the pickup into Neutral and pulled hard on the steering wheel, using the downhill slope to get her off the blacktop and into the roadside grass, where she shuddered to a standstill. He stroked the padded dash. "You'll be safe here."

But Zach would not. It was getting dark, and it was already too damn cold for his cowboy ass. Zach's battered body was a barometer, and he was feeling South Dakota, big time. He'd have given his right arm to be climbing into a hotel hot tub instead of a brutal blast of north wind. The right was his free arm anyway. Damn thing had lost altitude, touched some part of the bull and caused him a scoreless ride last time out.

It wasn't scoring him a ride this night, either. A carload of teenagers whizzed by, topping off the insult by laying on the horn as they passed him. It was at least twenty minutes before another vehicle came along. He stepped out and waved both arms this time, damn near getting himself killed. Whatever happened to *do unto others?* In places like this, decent people didn't leave each other stranded in the cold.

His face was feeling stiff, and he figured he'd better start walking before his toes went numb. He struck out for a distant yard light, the only sign of human habitation in sight. He couldn't tell how distant, but he knew he'd be hurting by the time he got there, and he was counting on some kindly old man to be answering the door. No shame among the lame.

It wasn't like Zach was fresh off the operating table—it had been a few months since his last round of repairs—but he hadn't given himself enough time. He'd lopped a couple of weeks off the near end of the doc's estimated recovery time, rigged up a brace, done some heavy-duty taping and climbed onto another bull. Hung in there for five seconds—four seconds past feeling the pop in his hip and three seconds short of the buzzer.

He could still feel the pain shooting down his leg with every step. Only this time he had to pick the damn thing up, swing it forward and drop it down again on his own.

Pride be damned, he just hoped *somebody* would be answering the door at the end of the road. The light in the front window was a good sign.

The four steps to the covered porch might as well have been four hundred, and he was looking to climb them with a lead weight chained to his left leg. His eyes were just as screwed up as his hip. Big black spots danced around with tiny red flashers, and he couldn't tell what was real and what wasn't. He stumbled over some shrubbery, steadied himself on the porch railing and peered between vertical slats.

There in the front window stood a spruce tree with a silver star affixed to the top. Zach was pretty sure the red sparks were all in his head, but the white lights twinkling by the hundreds throughout the huge tree, those were real. He wasn't too sure about the woman hanging the shiny balls. Most of her hair was caught up on her head and fastened in a curly clump, but the light captured by the escaped bits crowned her with a golden halo. Her face was a soft shadow, her body a willowy silhouette beneath a long white gown. If this was where the mind ran off to when cold started shutting down the rest of the body, then Zach's final worldly thought was, *This ain't such a bad way to go.*

If she would just turn to the window, he could die looking into the eyes of a Christmas angel.

* * * * *

*Could this woman from Zach's past get the lonesome
cowboy to come in from the cold...for good?
Look for
ONE COWBOY, ONE CHRISTMAS
by Kathleen Eagle
Available December 2009
from Silhouette Special Edition®*

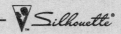

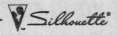

SPECIAL EDITION

**FROM *NEW YORK TIMES* AND *USA TODAY*
BESTSELLING AUTHOR**

KATHLEEN EAGLE

ONE COWBOY,
One Christmas

When bull rider Zach Beaudry appeared
out of thin air on Ann Drexler's ranch,
she thought she was seeing a ghost of
Christmas past. And though Zach had
no memory of their night of passion years
ago, they were about to share a future
he would never forget.

*Available December 2009
wherever books are sold.*

SSE65493

Visit Silhouette Books at www.eHarlequin.com

REQUEST YOUR FREE BOOKS!
2 FREE NOVELS PLUS 2
FREE GIFTS!

Love, Home & Happiness!

YES! Please send me 2 FREE Harlequin® American Romance® novels and my 2 FREE gifts (gifts are worth about $10). After receiving them, if I don't wish to receive any more books, I can return the shipping statement marked "cancel." If I don't cancel, I will receive 4 brand-new novels every month and be billed just $4.24 per book in the U.S. or $4.99 per book in Canada.* That's a savings of close to 15% off the cover price! It's quite a bargain! Shipping and handling is just 50¢ per book. I understand that accepting the 2 free books and gifts places me under no obligation to buy anything. I can always return a shipment and cancel at any time. Even if I never buy another book from Harlequin, the two free books and gifts are mine to keep forever.

154 HDN EYSE   354 HDN EYSQ

Name	(PLEASE PRINT)

Address	Apt. #

City	State/Prov.	Zip/Postal Code

Signature (if under 18, a parent or guardian must sign)

Mail to the Harlequin Reader Service:
IN U.S.A.: P.O. Box 1867, Buffalo, NY 14240-1867
IN CANADA: P.O. Box 609, Fort Erie, Ontario L2A 5X3

Not valid to current subscribers of Harlequin® American Romance® books.

Want to try two free books from another line?
Call 1-800-873-8635 or visit www.morefreebooks.com.

* Terms and prices subject to change without notice. Prices do not include applicable taxes. N.Y. residents add applicable sales tax. Canadian residents will be charged applicable provincial taxes and GST. Offer not valid in Quebec. This offer is limited to one order per household. All orders subject to approval. Credit or debit balances in a customer's account(s) may be offset by any other outstanding balance owed by or to the customer. Please allow 4 to 6 weeks for delivery. Offer available while quantities last.

Your Privacy: Harlequin is committed to protecting your privacy. Our Privacy Policy is available online at www.eHarlequin.com or upon request from the Reader Service. From time to time we make our lists of customers available to reputable third parties who may have a product or service of interest to you. If you would prefer we not share your name and address, please check here. ☐

HAR09R

Coming Next Month

Available December 8, 2009

Whether you want to surround yourself with baubles and bells
or dream of escaping to a warmer climate,
you can with Harlequin® Romance this Christmas.

#4135 AUSTRALIAN BACHELORS, SASSY BRIDES
Margaret Way and Jennie Adams
Two billionaire businessmen, used to calling the shots, are about to
meet their match in the burning heart of Australia. Watch the sparks fly
in these two stories in one exciting volume.

#4136 HER DESERT DREAM Liz Fielding
Trading Places
After trading places with Lady Rose, look-alike Lydia is leaving her job
at the local supermarket behind and jetting off to Sheikh Kalil's desert
kingdom!

#4137 SNOWBOUND BRIDE-TO-BE Cara Colter
Innkeeper Emma is about to discover that the one thing not on her
Christmas list—a heart-stoppingly handsome man with a baby in tow—
is right on her doorstep!

#4138 AND THE BRIDE WORE RED Lucy Gordon
Escape Around the World
Olivia Daley believes the best cure for a broken heart is a radical
change of scenery. Exotic, vibrant China is far enough from rainy, gray
England to be just that!

#4139 THEIR CHRISTMAS FAMILY MIRACLE Caroline Anderson
Finding herself homeless for the holidays, single mom Amelia's
Christmas wish is granted when she's offered an empty picture-perfect
country house to stay in. Then owner Jake steps through the door…

#4140 CONFIDENTIAL: EXPECTING! Jackie Braun
Baby on Board
Journalist Mallory must expose the secrets of elusive radio talk-show
host Logan. As their relationship goes off the record, Mallory is stunned
to discover she's carrying her own little secret….

HRCNMBPA1109